D1021998

THE SHIP of LOST SOULS

THE GUARDIANS of ISLAND X

THE SHIP of LOST SOULS

THE GUARDIANS of ISLAND X

2

by Rachelle Delaney

Grosset & Dunlap
An Imprint of Penguin Group (USA) Inc.

GROSSET & DUNLAP
Published by the Penguin Group
Penguin Group (USA) Inc., 375 Hudson Street,
New York, New York 10014, USA
Penguin Group (Canada), 90 Eglinton Avenue East, Suite 700,
Toronto, Ontario M4P 2Y3, Canada
(a division of Pearson Penguin Canada Inc.)
Penguin Books Ltd., 80 Strand, London WC2R 0RL, England
Penguin Group Ireland, 25 St. Stephen's Green, Dublin 2, Ireland
(a division of Penguin Books Ltd.)
Penguin Group (Australia), 250 Camberwell Road,
Camberwell, Victoria 3124, Australia
(a division of Pearson Australia Group Pty. Ltd.)
Penguin Books India Pvt. Ltd., 11 Community Centre,
Panchsheel Park, New Delhi—110 017, India
Penguin Group (NZ), 67 Apollo Drive, Rosedale,
Auckland 0632, New Zealand
(a division of Pearson New Zealand Ltd.)
Penguin Books (South Africa) (Pty.) Ltd., 24 Sturdee Avenue,
Rosebank, Johannesburg 2196, South Africa

Penguin Books Ltd., Registered Offices:
80 Strand, London WC2R 0RL, England

Text copyright © 2010 by Rachelle Delaney. Map illustration copyright © 2010
by Fiona Pook. Illustrations copyright © 2012 by Penguin Group (USA) Inc.
First published in Canada in 2010 as *The Lost Souls of Island X*
by HarperCollins Canada. First published in the United States in 2012 by
Grosset & Dunlap, a division of Penguin Young Readers Group,
345 Hudson Street, New York, New York 10014. GROSSET & DUNLAP
is a trademark of Penguin Group (USA) Inc. Printed in the U.S.A.

Library of Congress Control Number: 2011043289

ISBN 978-0-448-45779-6 (pbk)   10 9 8 7 6 5 4 3 2 1
ISBN 978-0-448-45778-9 (hc)   10 9 8 7 6 5 4 3 2 1

For Raine Penning,
pirate girl in the making.

CHAPTER ONE

Scarlet McCray was beginning to regret going barefoot. At the time, it had seemed like a jolly idea. After all, her feet hadn't even known a stocking for the first five years of her life. So why, she'd reasoned, confine her toes to some rat-eaten boots now that she was back in the place of her birth?

Except that now as she crept through the jungle, twigs snapping under her heels and burrs burrowing between her toes, she suspected she'd been too hasty in handing them off to that monkey who'd eyed them hopefully.

Maybe it was the funny kink in his long black tail. Or the way his fur stood up on one side of his head, like he'd just rolled out of bed. Whatever it was, Scarlet had been charmed into trusting him.

"But look, Monkey," she'd said as she tugged the boots off her feet, "you've got to take good care of these. I'll need them next time we set off on the *Hop* for a supply run."

The monkey had responded by snatching up the boots, pinching his nose, and scampering off, leaving Scarlet to wonder if she'd ever actually see them again.

She pushed aside a massive fern and climbed over a rock nearly as big as herself. Then she stopped to concentrate. At first she felt nothing, but after a few moments . . . yes, there it was. A faint tremor. And if she stood perfectly still and squeezed her eyes shut, she could feel something else. Uncertainty. Panic. Somewhere on the island, there were animals in distress. And it was up to her to find them.

Unfortunately, in a place like Island X, so full of surprises, this was no easy job.

It had only been a month since Scarlet and her crew had first set foot on the X-shaped island, but in that time she'd made more amazing discoveries than she had in her entire life. To start, she'd realized that Island X was, in fact, her birthplace. Scarlet was part Islander—one of the only remaining members of a culture killed off when people from the Old World came to the islands, bringing diseases and despair. Perhaps even the *only* remaining member.

And if that weren't overwhelming enough, she'd also discovered that somehow she was able to channel the island's animals and feel what they were feeling. If a flock of parrots rejoiced in the fruit of a nearby tree, her heart felt light and joyful. If the chief of the local band of smelly wild pigs had slept badly the night before, she felt that, too. It was a huge honor, an amazing ability. Not to mention totally perplexing.

The problem was, she could never tell when an animal in distress needed her help. Just an hour ago, for example, she'd followed a panicky feeling to its source, only to find the monkey with the kink in his tail having a temper tantrum because his brother had stolen his breakfast of termites. (He quickly got over it when she agreed to lend him her boots.)

Then, as soon as he'd left, she'd channeled another upset feeling. This one, she was fairly certain, came from the aras, her very favorite kind of bird. And while it was possible the aras were simply being harassed by hummingbirds, it was also possible that they were trying to warn her of something far more important. Like, for instance, a troop of treasure-hungry pirates. So she had no choice but to search for them—which was what she was doing now.

"If only I knew where I was," Scarlet grumbled, looking around the jungle with her fists on her hips. She concentrated hard. It was like a game of Hot and Cold, which the Lost Souls sometimes played on board the *Margaret's Hop*. Someone would hide a "treasure"— usually a lime or a piece of hardtack—while someone else would get blindfolded. Then the crew would yell "Hotttt!" or "Cooold!" as the blind one wandered toward or away from the treasure. In Scarlet's case, though, the feeling of distress grew stronger the closer she came to the anxious animal.

It felt strongest over to her left, but as she took a step in that direction, her foot sank right into a patch of amber-colored mud. "Blasted boots," she growled as the mud oozed between her toes. "And blasted monkey."

Trying to ignore her mucky foot, she inched toward some soft, leafy shrubs. "Maybe if I just cut through here . . ." Scarlet slipped between the shrubs, pushed through a wall of ferns, and found herself standing underneath the trees that held the aras' nests. Exactly where she wanted to be.

"But how . . . ?" She looked up into the tree branches and sighed. Her new talent was just one of many things about this island that she didn't understand. Its geography was another. Not for the first time, she wished her crew's only map hadn't been stolen by the treasure-hungry pirates. But then, she reminded herself for what must have been the millionth time since they'd landed on the island, what kind of Islander needs a map?

"An Islander who was forced to forget all about her island, that's who," she muttered.

When Scarlet was five years old, the Island Fever had struck her village, and her Islander mother had fallen ill. She'd begged her husband, a former admiral for the King's Men, to take Scarlet off the island and keep her healthy. Scarlet never saw her mother again.

Her father, John McCray, had returned to the King's Men, leaving Scarlet with a governess named Mary Lewis (aka Scary Mary), who'd made every attempt to erase Scarlet's memories of her old life. She'd even forced her to do awful things like curl her hair and wear petticoats and learn English.

Not that the English lessons themselves were awful. It was being forced to forget her language that truly scuttled. Now, with no other Islanders around, Scarlet doubted it would ever come back to her.

She studied the tree branches above her until she spotted a sparkle of red. Then she concentrated hard. The aras' distress was gone.

"Figures."

Scarlet grasped a low branch and swung herself up

into the nearest tree. She could climb it blindfolded by now. High above the ground, she settled into her usual spot on a sturdy branch and looked around. To her left she could see the clearing where the Lost Souls were camped. To her right stood another tree and another beyond it. And in those trees sat dozens of birds' nests—a rookery, the Old Worlders called it. And in those birds' nests sat dozens of sleepy scarlet-red birds with bands of green and blue on their wings. The aras. They didn't look a bit distressed.

"Well?" she said. "What was all that fuss about? Hummingbirds? Rotten fruit? Come on, I came all this way for *nothing*?"

A few aras eyed her drowsily, fluffed up their feathers, and went back to sleep.

"Honestly." Another problem, as she'd recently discovered, was that while she could understand what the animals were feeling, she had no way to communicate with them. No matter how much time Scarlet spent with them, the aras never seemed to understand a word she said.

A beam of sunlight sneaked through the tree canopy, illuminating specks of red in each nest, and despite her annoyance Scarlet couldn't help but smile. All these years, the King's Men and the pirates had been scouring the islands for treasure, as well as wood and spices, but they'd rarely come across a single jewel. Perhaps because the aras hid them so well. The birds simply scraped the ground with their beaks, nabbed the rubies here and there, and tucked them into the walls of their nests for safekeeping.

The King's Men, meanwhile, continued hunting the aras to near extinction for their gorgeous red feathers, not realizing that the birds were the key to the treasure they so desperately searched for.

Scarlet leaned back against the tree trunk and sighed. It was a funny situation, but not laugh-out-loud funny. The kind of funny that made you want to spit.

She turned away from the birds to look down on the Lost Souls' camp. It wasn't the place she'd originally called home; she had yet to find the spot where the Islanders' village once stood, although she guessed it was about an hour's journey from here. This clearing, with its long, soft grass and glistening freshwater pool, was a special place the Islanders used to visit a few times a year to relax, chat with neighbors, and harvest food and spices. It had a safe and peaceful feeling about it, which lingered even now, years after the last Islanders had been here. Scarlet was fairly certain they were still here in spirit, though. Island X was rumored to be one of *those* islands, filled with spirits and spooks that kept the pirates and King's Men far from its shores. Scarlet believed it was just the Islanders continuing to protect their home.

If she concentrated hard enough, she could picture the clearing as it had looked years ago—with children playing tag around the pool while their parents talked and filled baskets with seeds to grind into spices. If she focused even harder, she could picture her mother among them, tall and graceful and beautiful. And if she was very lucky, she could make out her father. Strong and relaxed and happy.

In a way, she'd not only lost her mother when the Island Fever hit, but her father, too. At least the father she knew and loved.

Once they'd left Island X, he rarely even paid her and Scary Mary a visit at the house where they lived in Jamestown. When he did, he was stern and stony. He refused to talk about the past and their life in the village or to call his daughter by her true name, Ara, which meant both a fiery shade of red and the brilliant bird of the same color.

Scarlet hadn't seen her father in nearly three years now, not since he'd announced that he was sending her to live with his family in the Old World. While Scarlet had been thrilled at the thought of escaping Scary Mary, she'd had no intention of spending the rest of her life in Old World ribbons and petticoats. So one afternoon, she'd up and run away. And it was a good thing, too, because if she hadn't, she'd never have met up with the Lost Souls or joined their jolly ship *or* been named their captain.

She squinted at the clearing. She could make out a few of the figures below: Liam and Ronagh Flannigan were playing catch with an enormous mushroom while Tim Sanders, the quartermaster of the *Margaret's Hop*, sat cross-legged near the pool, reading a thick book he'd lugged up from the ship. Other Lost Souls played Smelly Wild Pig in the Middle on the grass, and still more swung upside down in a nearby tree, screeching like monkeys.

From afar, Scarlet thought, they looked like normal Lost Souls. But she knew better. Her crew had been acting a little off since she'd made the "new mission" announcement a few weeks back. She felt their uncertainty as clearly as she'd felt the aras' anxiety or the monkey's outrage over his stolen breakfast.

It wasn't that the Lost Souls didn't want to protect Island X. But leaving the *Hop* to guard a treasure on land wasn't exactly the kind of mission they were used to. They'd grown accustomed to life at sea, dressing up like ghouls in black cloaks and raiding the ships of pirates and King's Men. And they probably could have carried on like that forever (or at least until they were grown up) if Jem Fitzgerald and his uncle Finn hadn't gotten themselves kidnapped by pirates. The Lost Souls had staged a rescue, and it turned out that Jem was in possession of a map to the storied treasure everyone was looking for. (Although no one knew quite what it was.) When he got separated from Uncle Finn, he joined the Lost Souls in a hunt for both the treasure and his uncle. A few jungle treks, bouts of treason on board the *Hop*, and battles with bloodthirsty pirates later, here they were, the guardians of Island X and all its treasures.

Scarlet only wished the Lost Souls could share her enthusiasm for the new mission. Maybe if she taught them more about the island, she mused, they'd feel more connected to it. But then, that would require her to remember all the details she'd forgotten in the past seven years. And at the rate she was remembering these days, that would take a while. She sighed again. It was all rather complicated.

"But don't you worry," she said, turning back to the aras, not caring if they understood English or not. "We'll protect the treasure from anyone who dares trespass. And not just the rubies. We're here to protect *all* of Island X."

She knew the Islanders would have appreciated that; it was this special, untouched place they'd valued, not some shiny red rocks. If the treasure hunters were to discover Island X's riches, they'd take not only every jewel on it, but also every tree and animal they pleased—just as they had on all the other islands.

"Don't you worry," Scarlet repeated, sounding far braver than she felt. "We've got a plan." She began to climb back down the tree to call the crew together to make that plan.

Scarlet had barely set foot in the clearing when she ran into eleven-year-old Jem Fitzgerald and his uncle Finn, who was supposedly a famous botanist on the other side of the world. Scarlet still thought that Finnaeus Bliss, with his very bald head and sweaty, egg-shaped body, looked nothing like a famous person should. But then, from what she'd heard, things were a little backward in the Old World.

"It's really the *Bediotropicanus onicus* that we're after," Uncle Finn was telling Jem, who seemed to be trying hard to stay awake. Uncle Finn tended to go on at length about plants. "It's one of the most riveting *Bedio*s I've heard of, and that's saying something! The structure of its anthers, you see—"

Scarlet decided that this was a fine time to interject and stepped toward them. "Are you off then, Uncle Finn?" He wasn't *her* uncle, of course, but all the Lost Souls had taken to calling him "Uncle Finn." They might never have admitted to missing their own parents, whom they'd either abandoned to join the Lost Souls or who'd abandoned them, but they were happy to take on a surrogate uncle.

Jem looked relieved at the interruption. Uncle Finn mopped his forehead with his handkerchief. "I am, indeed, Captain. Off on the trail of a plant that could change our lives."

Scarlet studied the sweaty scientist. Uncle Finn could be a little dramatic when it came to plants, but this sounded interesting. "Really? What is it?"

"A bromeliad."

"Oh." Scarlet herself wouldn't have known a bromeliad to see one, but she knew better than to admit that to Uncle Finn.

"A bromeliad that will"—he paused for effect—"cure the world of androgenetic alopecia."

Scarlet's eyes widened. "Really?"

Jem raised an eyebrow at her. "Do you know what that is?"

She shook her head. "Not a clue. But it sounds terrible."

"It is," Uncle Finn said solemnly.

"It's baldness," Jem said, blowing a lock of hair out of his eyes. "Hair loss."

"Oh." Scarlet looked from Jem to his uncle. "A bromeliad can cure that?"

Uncle Finn nodded. "I believe so. It'll take some

searching, though. And some intense experimentation. Fortunately, I've acquired a research assistant," he said, just as a monstrous man in tattered trousers came running toward them.

"Finn! Finn, I'm ready!" the man shouted. A cutlass hanging from his belt slapped his tree-trunk leg as he ran.

"Thomas?" Scarlet looked at Jem, who grinned.

The giant Thomas skidded to a stop in front of them, gasping for breath. "Thought . . . thought ye'd left without me. I was worried there."

Uncle Finn reached up to pat Thomas's shoulder. "I wouldn't leave without you, Thomas. I was just saying a few words to Jem before we go."

"Right. Course. I was . . . I was just worried."

Scarlet, Jem, and Uncle Finn all smiled at him. It was hard to believe that just a month ago Thomas had actually helped the treasure-hungry pirates kidnap Jem and Uncle Finn. It hadn't been his idea, of course—he'd worked on the *Dark Ranger*, a pirate ship captained by a nasty, rodentlike man with a very long name that Scarlet could never remember. But Thomas had proven himself a hero twice: first when he'd smuggled Uncle Finn off the ship and later when Captain What's-his-name had gotten his hands on the treasure map and intercepted the Lost Souls and Uncle Finn on Island X. There, beside the island's steamy Boiling Lake, Thomas had denied his captain's orders to do away with the children and taken their side instead.

Scarlet sighed happily at the memory. Thomas was a jolly pirate. She'd miss him while he was off on this new adventure, but she could tell he was happy as a clam to be a real research assistant.

"Now, Jem, Scarlet." Uncle Finn stuffed his handkerchief in his pocket. "We'll be gone a few days. And I wouldn't be a good uncle if I didn't say this."

"Uncle Finn, we—" Jem began to protest.

"Quiet, boy. We've seen many dangers on this island—"

"But—" Scarlet interjected, ready to assure him that she was well aware of all the dangers. Uncle Finn stopped her with a wave of his hand.

"*But* we've been here a month, and all seems well. Plus, I know the Lost Souls are capable of taking care of themselves. Lord knows if you can sail a ship and raid schooners without getting caught, you can camp alone on an island. *However*, you mustn't forget the dangers. Yes, the animals might be on your side. Yes, the spirits seem to be looking out for you. But the Dread Pirate Captain Wallace Hammerstein-Jones—"

"*That's* his name!" Scarlet exclaimed, and received a glare from Uncle Finn. "Sorry. I just . . . it's a long name," she murmured.

Finn cleared his throat. "You mustn't forget about Captain Wallace. He has our old map, and he'll be back. So promise me you'll be careful."

Scarlet and Jem mumbled their promises.

"Good. And if you need me, I won't be far away. In fact . . ." He reached into his pocket and pulled out a funny little pipe about the size of Scarlet's pinkie finger. "I'll leave this with you. It looks harmless, but believe me, it will shatter the nearest eardrum. If you need me"—he tossed Jem the pipe—"just call."

"All right." Jem tucked it in his pocket.

"Well then. Thomas, if you're ready."

Thomas straightened and saluted. "At yer service, Cap'n Finn."

Uncle Finn shook his head. "Just Finn, Thomas. We're off then. Take care, you two."

"We will," Scarlet and Jem chorused. They followed the researchers to the edge of the clearing, then stood and waved until they disappeared behind the curtain of leaves and vines.

CHAPTER TWO

"All good pirates come to order!"

Scarlet surveyed the twenty-two scruffy, sunburned children before her. They looked up expectantly from their places on the grass. The twins, Emmett and Edwin, were passing around slices of juicy orange papaya. Scarlet paused for a moment to remember that, not long ago, all they'd had to snack on were a few jawbreaking lumps of hardtack. She couldn't say she missed that part of the pirate life.

"All right, crew, it's time we got organized. First item on the agenda . . . yes, Ronagh?"

Ronagh Flannigan, one of the youngest Lost Souls at eight years old and the only other girl in the crew, dropped her hand in her lap. "I'm wondering . . . you said, 'All good pirates,' and, well . . . *are* we still pirates, Scarlet?"

"Course we're still pirates," Tim piped up. "We still have a ship." The quartermaster's love of nautical knowledge had long ago earned him the nickname Drivelswigger, or Swig for short.

"But we're barely ever on the ship," Monty, a boy with enormous feet, pointed out. The rest of the crew erupted into chatter.

"*I'm* still a pirate!"

"But technically you're not."

"Am *too*!"

"Wait!" Scarlet cried. "Quiet, everyone! I said quiet!" The Lost Souls fell silent. "Of course we're still pirates. We're too good at being pirates to not be pirates. But we're . . . we're more than pirates now. We're the guardians of a treasure. We're . . ." She paused, searching for a good word.

"Island warriors," thirteen-year-old Smitty finished, a dreamy gleam in his eyes. Smitty was one of the few Lost Souls who was truly excited about their new home. Actually, he seemed most excited about creating "island warrior" costumes with jungle plants. He also came up with warrior names to match them.

The Lost Souls still didn't know Smitty's real name; when he'd first boarded the *Margaret's Hop* he'd told them that no good pirate would go by the awful name his parents, the Smiths, had given him. Sometimes the crew called out terrible names like Horace or Leander— just to see if he'd answer.

"Right. Something like that," Scarlet said. She knew she hadn't *really* answered the question, but it was a tricky one, and she needed time to think about exactly how to define the Lost Souls now. It also wasn't as important as deciding how to fight off the pirates when they returned to the island. "So, first item on the agenda . . . yes, Fitz?"

Jem lowered his hand and cleared his throat. "I say we talk about housing. I mean, it's all well and good to sleep under the stars, and I know the animals won't hurt us here, but we'll need better cover than our cloaks when it rains."

A few pirates nodded and murmured their agreement.

Scarlet had to admit Jem was right. Sleeping under the stars was jolly, but sleeping in the rain would seriously scuttle, and it was bound to happen sooner or later. Jem was full of practical Old World ideas like that. He was another one of the few who didn't seem fazed by their new home. But Jem hadn't had time to get used to life on the *Hop* before they'd moved to Island X, Scarlet reasoned. To him, everywhere and everything was new and exciting.

But Scarlet was reluctant to start building shelters in a place that was obviously so special. The Islanders, she was certain, used to only visit the clearing where the Lost Souls were camped to make sure it stayed unspoiled. She told Jem as much.

"I thought you'd say that," he said. "And I have a solution. Tree houses!"

"Tree houses! What fun!" Smitty shouted.

"It's more than fun, though," said Jem. "We'll build them on the edge of this clearing, so we can keep watch over it without harming it. And most importantly, it'll be a good battle tactic. From up high we'll be able to spot invaders before they find us."

Scarlet liked that. "Does anyone know how to build a tree house?"

"I bet I could figure it out," Jem offered. "We did some woodwork back at the King's Cross." The King's Cross School for Boys had been Jem's boarding school in the Old World. "And Emmett and Edwin are good at that kind of thing."

The twins looked at each other and shrugged. Scarlet recalled the time they'd tried to fix a few loose boards on the *Hop*; Edwin had nailed his brother's pant leg to the ship, then hammered his own thumb with such gusto that he'd declared himself unfit to clean the long drop (as the Lost Souls called the toilet) for an entire month. But Jem looked so hopeful, so ready to put his Old World knowledge of things like fractions and right angles to good use.

"Go to it, then. Jem, you'll head up the Housing Committee."

Jem's ears turned pink with pride. "Thank you," he murmured.

"You're welcome."

Scarlet was about to move on to the subject of pirate attacks when Monty suggested they form a committee for food gathering. Scarlet agreed that was a good idea, too. While her crew may have been uneasy about living on land, they were certainly good at preparing to do it. "Who wants to lead it?"

She saw Gil Jenkins's hand shoot up but instead chose a reliable though rather unimaginative boy named Charlie. Gil had been Lucas Lawrence's sidekick before Lucas defected to join the *Dark Ranger* pirates—with Jem's treasure map. Scarlet still didn't trust him entirely, even now that Lucas was gone. She often gave him tasks that kept him closer to home rather than the ones he wanted. She knew the boy didn't appreciate it, but he had, after all, planned to mutiny against her.

"You can pick your own crew of food gatherers,"

she told Charlie. "You'll collect things like star fruit and guava—"

"And nuts," Ronagh added.

"Papaya," Emmett said over a mouthful of it.

"Berries," said Monty.

"Wild pigs," said Sam, the mouth-breather.

There was a pause as twenty-two heads turned to the boy with perpetual sniffles. Then Ronagh screeched, *"Wild pigs?"*

"You know . . . for meat?" Sam's eyes darted around, looking for support.

"We're not *eating* the *pigs*!" Ronagh's face turned red beneath her freckles. "Are we, Scarlet?"

"No, no, of course not," Scarlet said. Though they smelled like dirty socks and rotten cheese, and though they did have a tendency to rip humans limb from limb, the local band of smelly wild pigs seemed to be on the Lost Souls' side. They'd protected them from Lucas and the *Dark Ranger* pirates when the intruders attacked. "We can't eat the pigs, Sam. They're our friends."

"Then what about the other animals?" Gil asked.

Scarlet looked around the group. Most Lost Souls were shaking their heads, but a few seemed to be considering it. Ronagh looked as if she might explode.

"No," she repeated firmly before the little girl could blow her ginger top. "I don't feel right about it. Remember how the monkeys and aras and snakes chased away the pirates? Let's stick to foods we can harvest for now. After a few weeks we can reassess the situation." She knew Jem would like that. Along with fractions, right angles, and asking far too many questions, assessing situations was one of his Old World specialties.

"Hmph." Ronagh stuck her tongue out at Gil.

Blimey, I'm being wishy-washy today, Scarlet thought. But the crew was throwing tough questions at her—questions that deserved some thought.

"All right, next item. How about—" Scarlet stopped as a feeling of distress cut right through her brain. Another animal in need. Not as impatient as a monkey or as nervous as a shrew . . . a snake, she decided. Possibly from the nearby pit of deadly striped vipers.

"What's wrong?" Jem asked.

"Oh, nothing." She'd ignore it. At least until after they'd decided how to fight off the pirates. "Next item . . . yes, Swig?"

"Captain, what about the *Hop*?" Tim straightened his spectacles. He'd stolen them from the Dread Pirate Captain What's-his-name when the Lost Souls first raided the *Dark Ranger*, and Scarlet had yet to see the boy without them perched on his nose. "I'm worried someone might steal her. We can't just leave her alone." The quartermaster shoved his hands in his pockets. For the past month, he'd led regular trips down to the ship to gather supplies and patrol the shores of Island X. Since it took a good five hours to reach the ship, the Lost Souls usually stayed overnight and hiked back up in the morning. The long trip never fazed the Drivelswigger, though. A real sea dog, Tim was—born to steer a ship. Unfortunately, that also made him the Lost Soul who felt least at home on Island X.

"D'ya think we really need it?" Smitty asked. "I mean, now that we live here, maybe we should just get rid of it."

Tim looked at Smitty the way Ronagh had just looked at Gil. "Get rid of the *Hop*? Are you *insane*?"

"No, we can't get rid of it," Scarlet hurried to say before Tim's eyes could get any bigger. The snake was still nagging at her brain. *Give me five minutes*, she tried to tell it. "The *Hop* is our home. Well, our other home. Swig, why don't you gather a group and find a good hiding place for it? Maybe a cove someplace close by? It's not the perfect solution, but it'll do for now."

Tim nodded. "It's the least we can do. I'll take Monty, Elmo, and . . ." He looked past Gil's waving hand. "Liam. Let's head out this afternoon."

"What about me? Can I come?" Gil asked, still waving his hand.

"Uh-uh," Tim replied. "It's best to have a small crew."

Gil dropped his hand and pouted.

"All right now. Final item for discussion." Knowing that this one might take a while, Scarlet settled cross-legged on the ground with the crew. "We don't know when Lucas and the pirates will return, but we know for sure they will. We can't let them get near the rubies, of course, but there could be trouble if they even see the clearing." She gestured to the trees and the shining pool. "We have to decide what we're going to do and how we'll fight them off."

A long pause ensued. Several of the Lost Souls became very interested in the grass.

"Tree house lookouts?" Jem suggested.

"That's a good start," said Scarlet. "What else?"

Another pause. Sam sniffed. Ronagh squirmed.

"What about the animals?" asked Elmo. "They helped us chase off the baddies before. I bet they'd do it again."

A few pirates nodded, looking hopeful.

Scarlet chewed her lip. The smelly wild pigs were the only animals on Island X that seemed to understand English. Jem himself had made that recent discovery. Scarlet had assumed it would make her job much easier, but she'd soon found that being able to understand her didn't seem to make the pigs any more willing to help.

"Maybe," she told the crew. "But I'm not sure we can depend on them all the time."

"Why wouldn't they want to help?" asked Liam. "This is their home."

Scarlet looked at her crew, debating how to tell them that whenever she spoke to the pig chief, she could feel a clear lack of enthusiasm.

Smitty jumped to his feet. "I can't think of a better time to cut in," he said. "Ladies and gentlemen of Island X, allow me to present . . . the island warrior uniform." With that, Smitty reached behind him, produced a large fern, and plopped it on his head.

For a moment the Lost Souls looked stunned. Then they burst into laughter.

"Nice hat, Bertrand!"

"Wait! This is fierce, not funny!" Smitty cried. "Think how well we'll blend in to the jungle when we attack that biscuit-eater, Lucas, and his filthy crew." He turned to

Scarlet, a hopeful look in his eyes. "Captain? What do you think?"

She wrinkled her nose. "I think you're wearing a plant on your head."

The Lost Souls howled. But Smitty just wagged a finger at them. "Watch." He crouched low to the ground. "We can hide in the bushes like this. And when Lucas arrives"—he hopped up again and pulled off his hat—"he'll be all, 'Look at me, here to steal the treasure, har har.' And then . . ." Smitty put the fern back on his head and crouched again. "We'll jump up like this. *Argh!*" He jumped up and waved his arms, nearly losing his fern. "And scare the bilge rat senseless. See?"

He pulled Liam up to act like Lucas. Liam pretended to weep like a baby while Smitty danced around with his new headpiece. The Lost Souls roared, imagining the traitor at Smitty's mercy.

Scarlet laughed, too, but halfheartedly. She'd lost their attention, and the snake's angst was still rattling in her brain. She gave in and stood up. *I'm coming, you impatient reptile*, she tried to tell it. *Keep your scales on.* "This meeting is adjourned, mates," she said aloud, although that was quite obvious since most of the Lost Souls were now dancing a jig around Smitty and Liam.

"At least they're acting more like the Lost Souls of the *Margaret's Hop*," she murmured as she walked away. But it was little consolation. They still had no plan to protect the island. And it was sure as the thorn in the sole of her foot, Lucas and his crew would be back.

CHAPTER THREE

Jem liked to envision his new title with capital letters: Head of the Housing Committee. It looked rather important like that.

After the meeting, he'd immediately gotten to work, collecting some thin palm bark, an ara feather (found under a nest and not plucked from the source, of course), and some bright purple berries. Then he'd crushed the berries into a thick juice. *Voilà!* He had paper, a quill, and ink to sketch the tree house village he was going to build.

It hadn't taken him long to realize, however, that he hadn't a clue how to build a tree house, let alone an entire village. Not that he'd been fibbing at the meeting; he had done some woodwork at the King's Cross School for Boys. And yet, he wasn't sure that carving a cricket bat was exactly on par with building a real house to hold real people. So he reassessed the situation and decided to start by choosing the best place to build the tree houses.

For that, he would need to draw a map.

He began by sketching the clearing, from the freshwater pool and the rookery to the papaya trees. Then he drew the rest of Island X, adding as many details as he could remember from his treks down to the *Hop* and from Uncle Finn's original map. He vaguely recalled that map warning of a panther's lair on the western arm and two dangerous mountain peaks to the north, so he sketched them in, hoping he'd never encounter them.

As he worked, he realized that his map could also help the other Lost Souls. They might feel more at home if they knew the lay of the land. Even Uncle Finn might like a copy! Jem kept his head down and sketched throughout the evening and most of the following day.

He'd just added the finishing touches to the compass in the corner and had leaned back against the tree that shaded him from the sticky-hot afternoon sun when Scarlet wandered by without even seeing him.

"Scarlet!" he cried.

"Fitz!" She leaped a good foot off the ground. "You just took a year off my life." She looked a little disheveled, with twigs sticking out of her hair and scratches on her cheeks. But then, Jem had never really seen the captain of the Lost Souls in any other state. Scarlet wasn't exactly the garden party type.

"Sorry, Captain." He scrambled to his feet. "But look what I've been working on." He presented his map with pride.

Scarlet looked at it blankly for a moment. "It's a map," she said.

"Well, yes, of course. I was going to draw up the plans for the tree houses, but then I decided to start with a map of the area."

Scarlet nodded, looking distracted. "It's . . . nice."

Jem's pride fizzled. "Well, it's not supposed to be *nice*," he huffed. "It's supposed to be accurate." He began to roll up his masterpiece.

"Oh, Fitz, I'm sorry," said Scarlet. "It's a great map. I'm just not thinking straight. I . . ."

Jem looked at her squarely. Something was obviously wrong. "Captain, what's going on?"

"Nothing. It's . . ." Scarlet met his eyes, then looked down at her bare feet. After a pause, she sighed. "All right, if you must know, it's this . . ." *How to explain without sounding loony?* Scarlet wondered. *"Ability* the island's given me. Don't get me wrong, I'm grateful for it. But . . . it's a little . . . overwhelming. Like having an entire zoo in your head. All the animals are hungry. Or too hot. Or regretting how much they ate last night."

Jem didn't entirely understand Scarlet's new talent. But it sounded somehow like every animal in and around the clearing could let Scarlet know how it was feeling, whether it was sad, happy, or suffering from indigestion. It wasn't the kind of talent Jem would want, no, sir.

"Take this monkey, for one," Scarlet continued. "He's always fussing, but it never turns out to be anything important. This morning, he took me on a wild goose, er, monkey chase all over the jungle just to show me why he was so darn upset."

"And?"

Scarlet plucked a twig out of her hair. "It was his brother. Again."

"Not Lucas Lawrence? Not Captain Wallace?"

"Not even. Just his brother being a copycat. You know how monkeys are, imitating everything you do. Well, this monkey's brother wouldn't stop copying him, and it was driving him crazy 'cause no matter what he

did, the brother would do the exact same thing, and—"
She stopped and crossed her arms over her chest. "You're looking at me like I'm loony."

"No, no. It's just . . . hard to believe," Jem replied.

"You're telling me. Sometimes I wish this guardian role came with instructions."

Jem nodded sympathetically.

Scarlet tugged on a tangled lock of hair. "It's also taking me away from more important matters like the pirates. Speaking of which, have you started building the tree houses yet?"

"Well, no. I told you, I decided to draw a map first. Look, I'll show you where I'm thinking of building them." He began to unroll the scroll again.

Scarlet nodded. "Sure. I just . . ." Then she rubbed her head. "Really? Again?" She squeezed her eyes shut. "This one's upset in a grouchy, sluggish kind of way—like it's been out in the sun too long. I bet it's an iguana."

"But . . . couldn't you just ignore it?" Jem asked, wondering what a sluggish and sunburned iguana felt like.

Scarlet opened her eyes. "Maybe. But then, what if it really is trying to tell me something important? I've been given this talent for a reason. And that's to protect the island." She paused, looking at Jem. "Right?"

"I suppose so," Jem said with a shrug.

"Right. Look, Fitz, I trust you one hundred percent. Choose a spot for the houses, then gather your team and start the construction. I'll check up on you as soon as I can. Right now I've got, you know . . ."

"I know. A job to take care of. Need a map?" Jem held it up.

For a moment, she looked as if she might accept it. Then she squared her shoulders, shook her head, and wandered off, muttering, "I'm coming. I'm coming."

Tim had a great mind for construction. Or rather, Tim had a great mind for ships and timbers, so Jem assumed that he'd be good at construction, too. He decided to seek out the quartermaster to talk tree houses.

Jem surveyed the clearing but could see no sign of Tim. He had left immediately after the previous day's meeting to find a hiding place for the *Hop*.

"He ought to be back by now," Jem muttered as he walked across the clearing, map tucked under his arm. "You'd think—"

"Lookin' for someone, mate?"

Jem looked around and found himself face-to-face with a purple-skinned boy.

"Argh!" he yelled. "What the flotsam?"

Smitty, naked except for a skirt of leaves that hung to his knees, had gone and painted his entire body a deep crimson purple. He grinned, and his teeth looked frighteningly white against his skin. "Ha! Fitz, you look like you're seeing a ghost!"

"I look like I'm seeing a crazy person!" Jem shot back. "What on earth are you doing?"

"Amazing transformation, isn't it?" Smitty spun around so Jem could admire the full picture.

"Oh, Smit, don't. Your . . . leaves . . ." Jem covered his eyes with his hands.

Smitty stopped spinning. "Whoops." He adjusted his leafy skirt. "But look! This paint is made from crushed berries. It's brilliant!"

"I know. I've been using it as ink, and look what happened." Jem showed Smitty his purple-stained fingers. "But, Smit, you painted yourself purple on purpose? Why?"

Smitty shrugged. "Just figured our island warrior uniforms needed a bit of color."

"Well, you're certainly colorful."

"I know. But it's not quite right." Smitty looked down at his skirt. "I think it needs a few adjustments."

Jem tried not to laugh. "I agree."

Smitty turned to leave, then turned back. "Say, Fitz, when did you crush those berries?" He pointed at Jem's purple fingers.

"Yesterday after the meeting. I tried washing it off, but no luck."

The corners of Smitty's mouth turned down, and his eyes widened. "No luck?"

Jem looked at Smitty's purple skin and laughed. Like it or not, Smitty was going to be quite colorful for days. "I hope you like purple." He walked away grinning.

At least Smitty wasn't acting out of sorts like some of the others, Jem noted. Tim, for instance—now there was a real lost soul. Jem picked up his pace, scanning the clearing for the quartermaster.

"Jem! Jem!"

He turned to see Edwin hurrying toward him. "Have you seen my dagger?" Edwin demanded.

"Um . . . I don't think so," Jem replied, trying to remember what Edwin's dagger looked like. "Where did you last have it?"

"I always keep it under my cloak, and today it's just . . . *gone*!" Edwin took a step closer and lowered his voice. "I've got a feeling someone took it."

"But who would steal . . . ?" Jem's voice trailed off as he remembered how Gil Jenkins had helped Lucas steal his own knife not long ago. The thought must have been written across his face because Edwin nodded grimly.

"I was just on my way to find Mr. Jenkins myself," he said. "I'll see you later." He stalked off before Jem could remind him that he had promised to help Jem build the tree houses.

Jem watched him go, thinking that this job as Head of the Housing Committee might be a lot harder than he'd thought. He wouldn't make much progress on construction if his helpers were off chasing lost weapons and hiding ships.

Fortunately, at that moment, a voice hollered, "We're back!" and Monty, Elmo, Liam, and Tim himself strolled into the clearing. All four Lost Souls looked sweaty and tired.

Jem trotted over to them. "Did you find a spot to hide the *Hop*?"

Liam nodded. "We found a little cove not far from here and tucked her in there."

"Here." Jem proudly unfurled his map. "Show me."

They *ooh*ed and *aah*ed for a moment, then Tim pointed out how they'd hiked down to retrieve the ship on the island's southern arm. Uncle Finn's old map had indicated they drop anchor there. Then they'd sailed it around to the cove between the north and east arms.

"We figured it'd be easier to hike straight up from the cove to get back to camp," Liam said. "But it turns out there's a reason why Uncle Finn's map said to hike in from the other side. We had to climb right up the cliffs! Took us a good four hours."

"It nearly killed me," Monty said and flopped dramatically on the grass.

Tim ignored them, focusing instead on Jem's map. "You should mark where the *Hop* is hidden now. That's important. If you want a good look, there's a spot not far from here where you can see her. Actually, I'm going to run out there now, just to check up on her," Tim said. "Wanna come?"

Liam looked at Tim as if he'd gone mad. "Swig, we spent the last four hours climbing a cliff! Aren't you tired?"

Tim shook his head. "I . . . I think I forgot to batten down the hatches. And . . . it might rain."

Liam and Jem looked up at the cloudless sky, then exchanged a glance. There was no doubt about it. Their quartermaster was a Lost Soul who would never feel entirely at home again with his boots planted on dry land.

"Suit yourself." Liam shrugged. "I'm going to have a snack and a nap." Monty grunted his agreement from the grass.

"You coming, Jem?" Tim asked.

"Sure," Jem replied. At least this would give him a chance to talk to Tim about tree houses.

As he trailed Tim down a skinny path that snaked through the trees, Jem wondered how the quartermaster was staying upright after his journey to hide the *Hop*. He decided he'd better get down to business before Tim passed out from exhaustion.

"Swig, I want to talk to you about the tree houses I'm going to build."

"I think she's lonely, Jem."

"You think who what?" Jem stopped.

"The *Hop*. I think she misses us." Tim quickened his pace.

"Tim," Jem puffed, trying to catch up, "the *Hop*'s a boat. Boats don't have feelings."

"Now see, that's where you're wrong," Tim called over his shoulder. "They *do* have feelings. Why, you should hear how creaky she's grown in just a month. I think she's depressed."

Jem decided not to point out that the *Hop* was a very old ship. She had served the Lost Souls well, but someday, possibly soon, she would need to be replaced. There was no convincing Tim right now, though. He obviously had a bad case of homesickness. Jem had felt just the same when his parents first left him at the King's Cross School for Boys. He hadn't, however, felt a speck of homesickness since he'd left the Old World. On the contrary, he tried his best not to make any mention of home around Uncle Finn in case it gave him any ideas of returning.

They hiked in silence for what Jem imagined was about fifteen minutes, until the trees suddenly thinned and the boys stumbled out onto a sunny plateau. The sea splayed before them, deep blue and dotted with whitecaps, and a warm wind wrapped them in the smell and taste of salt.

"There she is." Tim smiled and pointed down to the left, where the *Hop* was tucked inside a narrow cove.

"Good work," Jem said. "It's very well hidden."

Tim sat down on the ground. "I hope so." He plucked a few blades of grass without taking his eyes off the ship. Finally he said, "Just between you and me, Jem, I miss the *Hop*."

"No. Really?" Jem feigned surprise.

"I know. I hide it well," said Tim. "And don't get me wrong. This place is jolly. And someone has to protect the treasure. But . . . when I'm on the *Hop*, I feel different. I feel *right*. The ocean's a part of me. I learned to steer a ship before I even learned to tie my bootlaces."

"Swig, you still can't tie your bootlaces." Jem pointed at the boy's laces, in knots rather than bows.

Tim looked down impatiently. "Bows are a complete waste of time. Anyway, I just want to be on the water. Like . . . like that ship out there. I want the salt and the spray—"

"Which ship?"

Tim waved his hand in the direction of the ocean. "That one. Even the hardtack. Jem, I actually like the dreadful stuff!"

Jem squinted into the sun.

"I like weighing anchor and—"

"Oh *no*."

"Although maybe not cleaning the long drop . . ."

"Tim! Tim, look!" Jem grabbed his friend's shoulder and pointed at the horizon.

"I know, mate, it's a . . ." He pushed his spectacles up higher on his nose. "A sh—oh *no!*"

It was not just any ship approaching Island X at full speed. It was a most familiar ship with a most familiar flag flapping madly atop its main mast. The boys looked at each other.

"Scurvy," they said together.

The *Dark Ranger* had returned.

CHAPTER FOUR

If bloodthirsty pirates had tried to attack the Lost Souls on the *Margaret's Hop*, the crew would have known exactly what to do. They'd have grabbed their cloaks and weapons and charged off to fight the swabs.

On Island X, however, they did no such thing. Jem ran through the clearing, shouting the news the way a paperboy would holler the day's headlines, and the Lost Souls responded by throwing up their arms in panic.

"They're back!"

"What do we do?"

"Everybody calm down," Jem shouted. "We have to think clearly. We—"

Scarlet's voice rose above his, powerful and commanding as ever. "To the pool, pirates! NOW!"

The Lost Souls fell silent and sprinted for the pool.

By now it was late in the day, and the sun's belly was just touching the treetops to the west. Jem consulted his map, did some quick calculations, and figured it would be nearly midnight by the time the pirates anchored and trekked up to the camp. That is, if they were brave enough to venture into the jungle at night. The pirates knew as well as the Lost Souls that Island X was one of *those* islands.

Jem slipped into the crowd next to Liam and Tim and watched Scarlet pace before them. Finally she stopped and looked up. Her face was pale and her lips pressed into a thin line.

"All right, crew. We knew this would happen. Swig, Fitz, how far off was the ship when you saw it?"

"Maybe an hour from the anchoring spot marked on their map, Cap'n," Tim replied. His voice broke on the last word, and he cleared his throat.

Scarlet nodded. "I wonder if they'll make the hike up tonight."

"Under the cover of darkness," Ronagh whispered theatrically.

Her brother shushed her.

"I doubt it," Smitty said. A few of the Lost Souls around him did double takes upon noticing his purple skin. "Cap'n Wallace is a big jellyfish. I'll bet they wait till dawn."

Smitty had a point. One of the first things Jem had learned about Captain Wallace was that the man thought himself much bigger and bloodthirstier than he really was. This wasn't to say he wasn't dangerous—he just preferred to leave the dirty work to his crew.

"All right. I've got a plan," Scarlet said. "I don't think the pirates will face the jungle in the dark, either, but we can't count on them to be yellow-bellies."

"Yeah," Gil Jenkins piped up. "They've got Lucas now, and he's not afraid of the dark."

Twenty-two pairs of eyes turned to glare at Gil.

"What?" The boy crossed his arms over his chest. "I'm just saying he's no yellow-belly."

"As I was saying," Scarlet continued. "We can't assume

that they'll stay on board the *Dark Ranger* till morning. But there's a lot at stake here, and not just the rubies. We can't let those bilge rats lay eyes on this clearing. So I say we leave here tonight and head them off near the Boiling Lake or even farther down the trail in the valley. If they don't arrive tonight, we'll be ready for them tomorrow. It'll just mean camping out in the jungle." Even Scarlet's voice wavered on this note. It was one thing to sleep in the peaceful clearing, but another thing altogether to spend the night elsewhere on Island X.

"But then what?" asked Monty. "When they show up, will we fight 'em?" He kicked the air halfheartedly with a big foot.

Scarlet shrugged. "We'll have to."

"The uniforms aren't ready yet," Smitty moaned.

The Lost Souls shuffled and shifted.

"Wait!" cried Liam. "What about Uncle Finn and Thomas?" He looked at Jem. "Where are they?"

Jem had no answer for that. Then he remembered. He had a pipe to call the explorers—right in his pocket. "I'll find out," he said.

"Good," said Scarlet. "And I'll ask the smelly wild pigs and the monkeys if they wouldn't mind helping us out like they did before. I hate bringing them into this, but . . . maybe just once more."

Jem felt a bit better hearing this. The pigs were fierce and the monkeys very obnoxious. They'd set the pirates on the run in mere seconds last time.

Everyone else seemed to brighten as well.

"I forgot about the pigs!"

"Of course they'll help us."

"I'll do what I can, crew," said Scarlet. "Gather your weapons before it gets too dark and meet back here. Be ready to hike." Then she looked down at her bare feet, grunted, and marched off.

The rest of the Lost Souls ran off to find their cutlasses and knives. Jem emptied his trouser pockets, pulling out some nuts, a wad of lint, the beautiful silver and ivory handled knife he'd stolen from a pirate named Deadeye Johnny, and, finally, Uncle Finn's pipe.

Uncle Finn had warned him that it could blast out an eardrum, so Jem moved away from everyone. He held the pipe between his lips while plugging his ears with his fingers and blew into it with all his might.

Nothing.

Not a sound.

Jem blew harder, until his own ears popped.

Still nothing.

He smacked his forehead. A faulty noisemaker. "Uncle Finn, how could you?" He jammed the pipe back into his pocket.

"I still can't find my dagger!" Edwin yelled. "Whoever took it had better fess up!"

Jem shook his head. "Good thing the animals are on our side. We are not ready for a fight." He pictured the tree houses that should have been built already and the Lost Souls ambushing Captain Wallace from above. But then, Scarlet was right about not letting the pirates get close to the clearing. Perhaps he could build houses at strategic points along the trail, too.

Jem's thoughts were interrupted by muttered curses in the bushes nearby. A moment later, Scarlet emerged, looking frustrated.

"Did you find Uncle Finn?" she asked.

Jem shook his head. "The pipe's faulty. Doesn't make a sound."

"Well, now we're in trouble," Scarlet said. "I couldn't find the pigs, either."

"What about the monkeys?"

"I found some monkeys. But I'm pretty sure they don't understand English."

"Really?" Jem's stomach tossed and turned as though he were on a ship instead of standing on solid ground. What were they going to do?

"Really. The one who borrowed my boots just ignored me when I asked him to give them back."

"Wait a minute. You gave your boots to a monkey?" Jem asked, incredulous. "Why?"

Apparently that was the wrong thing to say. Scarlet pierced him with a cutlass glare, then stomped off. Jem sighed. If only Uncle Finn were there to help. And Thomas. The giant would give them the strength they needed to take on a shipload of cutlass-wielding pirates. He gulped. How on earth would they stand a chance?

The other Lost Souls looked as though they were wondering the same thing as they set off down the dark trail. It was the only one on Island X they knew fairly well, having followed it to the treasure in the first place. Out in front, Scarlet held a lantern brought up from the *Hop*, but near the back of the line, where Jem found himself, there was nothing but the odd firefly to light the way.

Over the past month, Jem had learned that the jungle was always much noisier at night than during the day. At night, it seemed as if every insect had something to say, and loudly. Some voices were high-pitched and squeaky and others deeper, like creaky wooden rocking chairs. Jem liked to imagine they were saying something like, "Dark tonight, isn't it?" "Sure is." "Hey, check out Mona's web!" "Ooh. Nice work!"

But on this night, the chorus seemed quieter, as if even the bugs understood the seriousness of the situation. A few bats flapped low overhead, and Jem wished he were closer to Scarlet so he could ask if they were trying to tell her something.

"It's too quiet," Smitty said suddenly. "I think it's time for . . ." And the Lost Souls' unofficial lyricist broke out into song.

Off we go to face some swabs.
Can't say that we're scared at all.
Off to face old Captain Wall'ce
and we're not scared.

They've got guns and cutlasses.
They've got broadswords and brute force.
They've speed, drive, and resolve.
But we're not scared.

If they take us prisoner,
hang us from the mizzenmast.
If they make us walk the plank . . .

"Smitty!"

The songster looked up at his captain, who'd stopped marching and was staring at him in disbelief.

"Maybe something a little more . . . uplifting?"

Several wide-eyed pirates murmured their agreement.

Smitty shoved his hands in his pockets. "Everyone's a critic."

As they passed the pit of deadly striped vipers (the "ophidian aggregation," as Uncle Finn called it), Scarlet slipped down into it to attempt to speak to the snakes. She emerged a few minutes later, shaking her head— apparently the snakes didn't understand English, either. She peeled a small one off her ankle, tossed it back into the pit, and continued marching down the trail. The Lost Souls followed, quiet once more.

They arrived at the Boiling Lake in darkness so deep and thick that it hid the rising steam. The Lost Souls knew exactly where they were, though. It was impossible not to, with sweat dribbling down their faces.

"Stay to the right, crew," Scarlet called. "The edge is just on your left."

Jem shuddered, thinking of the long fall down into burbling water. Like falling into a giant pot of soup.

Soup. His stomach rumbled, and he wondered if anyone had thought to bring snacks. He certainly hadn't.

The Lost Souls pushed on toward the nearby Valley of Simmering Streams. Even in the morning light, they'd barely be able to find one another in the steam rising from the Boiling Lake; the pirates would sneak right up on them before they knew it.

As they trudged on down the trail, Jem tried to distract himself by looking for details to add to his map. He noted a tree with roots as high as his forehead lying on top of the ground. He also noted that if he looked closely enough at the vegetation around him, dozens of tiny silver eyes would glimmer, then disappear.

He shivered. Perhaps this was best done in broad daylight.

Think happy thoughts, he told himself. Like Christmas pudding. Or booting a football clean past the goalkeeper in a tied game. Yes, that was good. Football matches rarely involved gleaming silver eyes.

He was so deep in thought that he didn't notice they'd arrived at the Valley of Simmering Streams until Scarlet announced, "We're here, crew."

They huddled around her lantern. Away from the lake, the air felt much cooler, and the sky glittered with millions of stars.

"I think we should camp close to the trees in case it rains. We'll take turns standing guard while the others sleep. Five patrollers at a time." She tapped the closest five heads. "Spread out along the valley and keep your eyes up." Scarlet gestured at the big hill in front of them. The pirates would have to climb up over the top before descending into the valley. The Lost Souls had slid down that very hill several times now. The slippery-slidey ride was always the best part of the trek into camp.

Jem found a dry spot on the ground near the edge of the trees and settled in, doubting that anyone would actually be able to sleep. If the moans and squeaks from the jungle didn't keep them awake, the knowledge that they would soon have to face the pirates surely would. Back on the *Hop*, they'd at least had their black cloaks to protect them—the pirates and King's Men had cowered at the sight of the little ghouls. But when Lucas had left, he'd blown their cover. Now his new crew knew that the Lost Souls were only children. They had nothing to hide behind anymore.

Jem leaned back on his elbows and looked up at the stars. He fell asleep trying not to think about how they reminded him of all those eyes in the jungle around him.

Jem awoke to a soft, steady clicking noise. He opened his eyes and for a moment assumed he was back in the clearing near the pool. Then he remembered and sat bolt upright. The stars had faded, and the sky was now a deep blue streaked with pink and violet. The clicking noise continued. Jem looked around for its source and found Emmett lying nearby, clacking his teeth in his sleep.

"Phew," he breathed, then wondered why no one had woken him for his night-watch shift. He glanced around the valley and saw a few patrollers on duty: Liam was drawing in the dirt with a stick while Ronagh chirped at a bird in a tree. But where were the others? Scarlet had said five would be on guard at a time. Jem stood and surveyed the bodies asleep on the ground around him. How had they all fallen asleep? How had he managed to fall asleep? And where was Scarlet?

Then Jem looked up at the hill.

He gasped as he took in one of the most terrifying things he'd ever seen.

Three faces stared down at him over the crest of the hill. One was blockish with dirty-brown hair and a nasty grimace. The next one was small with a pointy rodent nose. And the third had a red bandana wrapped too tightly around his dark hair. Lucas Lawrence. The Dread Pirate Captain Wallace Hammerstein-Jones. And Iron "Pete" Morgan, the captain's right-hand man.

The air was so still that Jem could hear Captain Wallace hiss, "Do you think he's seen us?"

Lucas didn't answer. Instead he hopped to his feet and waved at something behind him. Suddenly there were twenty—no, *forty* more pirates on top of the hill. Together they took a breath, then let out a big, bloodthirsty battle call.

"Everybody up! They're here! The pirates are here! SCARLET!" Jem screamed.

The Lost Souls leaped up from the ground, hollering and fumbling for their cutlasses. The pirates atop the hill roared again, but Jem could barely hear them. His own cries of "Scarlet! Captain!" drowned them out.

He found Tim searching for his spectacles in the grass.

"Where is she?"

"I don't know!" Tim found the glasses and settled them on his nose. "What do we do?"

Jem had no idea. He looked back to the top of the hill. There seemed to be some delay. Pete and Lucas Lawrence looked like they were arguing, while Captain Wallace was flapping his arms like a crazed parakeet.

"Let's block the trail," said Tim. "If we're spread all over the valley like this, the pirates'll just run by us and up the path."

"Right. Of course." Jem turned and sprinted through the crowd of Lost Souls, passing on Tim's instructions. On the hilltop, Lucas threw himself down on his stomach and began to barrel headfirst down the mountain. Even from a hundred yards away, Jem could see the wild look on his face. One by one, the *Dark Ranger* pirates began to slide down the hill behind him.

"To the trail!" Jem called and made a dash for it.

"We've got them on the run!" Captain Wallace crowed. "After them!"

The Lost Souls halted at the mouth of the trail and looked back, puffing and shivering. It was a horrifying sight—dozens of pirates sliding down the hill, cutlasses clamped between their teeth. And one wicked boy out in front, hollering curses the Lost Souls had never even heard before.

"We're in for it," whispered Sam.

What would Scarlet do? Jem wondered. Before a raid, she always wished the crew a peaceful death rather than the nasty one that might well await them. But Jem didn't think it was really the time for that. Lucas had slid to a halt at the bottom of the hill and was picking himself up, ready to charge.

Liam reached for his sister. "Get behind me, Ronagh!"

Emmett called, "It's been jolly knowing you all!"

Just then, there was a loud crash in the bushes behind them.

"We're here!" Scarlet hollered as she tumbled out of the bushes and onto her knees in the dirt. The Lost Souls let out a collective cry of relief as their captain, from down on all fours, looked up at the hill. Her mouth fell wide open, but whatever curses came out couldn't be heard, for a pack of smelly wild pigs was galloping past her, followed by about a dozen scampering monkeys and a pandemonium of parrots. The entire brigade charged right to the foot of the hill as the pirates, who'd lost their cutlasses when their jaws dropped at the sight, dug their fingernails into the ground to stop their slide. Their battle cries turned to shrieks of terror as the pigs lowered their tusks and ran right up the hill, tossing pirates aside as if they weighed no more than small root vegetables. Even Lucas screamed as a cloud of rhinoceros beetles flew out of the jungle and swarmed around his head. The boy spun around and ran right back up the hill along with all the other pirates. Captain Wallace was long gone, leading the sprint back to the *Dark Ranger*.

Within moments, every pirate had disappeared. Their footsteps faded away until all was still again, and morning proceeded to dawn as usual on Island X.

Smitty was the first to break the stunned silence. "Hurray!" he shouted, raising his fists as if he'd just won a race. A few others joined in the cheering.

"The animals *did* come," Liam cried. "Scarlet, how'd you do it?"

Scarlet finally got to her feet. "I searched for most of the night. They were downwind and hard to find. But I explained the situation, and they agreed it was important. On the way here, the pig chief rounded up some other animals to help out."

"The rhinoceros beetles were a nice touch," said Edwin.

"I am never eating meat again!" Ronagh vowed, and shook her finger at everyone around her. "*No one* is!"

No one argued. A few Lost Souls started to dance a victory jig. Others began to imitate the pirates upon seeing the animals.

But Jem stayed quiet. He couldn't help but wonder what would have happened if Scarlet hadn't found the pigs and shown up at just the right time. And he could tell by the look on his captain's face that she was thinking the very same thing.

CHAPTER FIVE

The path back to camp smelled of dirty socks and rotten cheese. But no one complained. All of a sudden, the smell of the wild pigs seemed quite tolerable indeed.

Every now and then Scarlet paused to channel the animals who'd chased away the pirates, but she felt nothing. Taking that as a good sign, she concentrated instead on what the flotsam the Lost Souls could do when the pirates returned—as they surely would.

Convincing the pigs to fight hadn't been easy. Actually, finding the pigs hadn't been a picnic, either. Scarlet had gotten herself hopelessly lost and would have likely still been wandering the jungle, sniffing for clues, if the island hadn't taken pity on her and plopped her right in the middle of the band of pigs.

The chief, a hairy barrel of a swine with wrinkly gray skin and an extremely long snout, had pulled back his lips and bared his pointy teeth when she began to plead her case. But they got on fairly well, she speaking aloud in English and he responding with easily read thoughts and feelings. He told her that while he knew the Lost Souls meant well, he wasn't keen on approaching a bunch of pirates that might serve up his crew for breakfast alongside their eggs.

"Don't do it for us," Scarlet whispered so as not to wake the rest of the pack. "Do it for the island. We're not just trying to protect the rubies. Everything on this island needs protecting—the trees and the aras and you, your band, and your children. If the pirates or anyone else get their dirty hands on this place, it'll be the end of Island X."

The pig chief snorted over this for a while, then woke his crew and gathered them for a meeting. After a great deal more grunting and a few clouds of seriously stinky air, the pigs turned to Scarlet, ready to follow her.

Never in her life had she felt so relieved.

As they'd crept through the darkness toward the valley, the chief had stopped here and there to recruit monkeys, parrots, and one very drowsy family of rhinoceros beetles. Scarlet considered asking the chief for tips on how to communicate with them herself but decided it wasn't the time.

Now as she led her crew back up the trail to camp, she wondered how they'd stand a chance if the pigs were ever to tire of helping them—and rallying the other animals. Scarlet smiled at the memory of those wonderful rhinoceros beetles shaking off their sleepiness just in time to fly right up Lucas's nose.

Then she frowned. Lucas would be back. And probably soon. She was in serious need of a plan.

By the time they reached camp, she was no closer to making one, and she was now also in serious need of a nap. Most of the Lost Souls seemed to agree; at least half headed right for their blankets and flopped face-first into the grass. The other half stumbled off to collect fruit and nuts for a midday meal. Scarlet yawned and decided that food could wait.

Halfway across the clearing, she stopped in her tracks. Someone was rummaging through the pile of belongings that marked her sleeping spot. Someone with a funny kink in his long black tail . . .

"MONKEY!"

She sprinted toward him. He looked up in surprise, shrieked, and dropped her cutlass. By the time she reached her things, he'd hightailed it into the trees.

"Honestly," Scarlet panted. "You give a monkey a boot, and he wants an entire ensemble." She checked to make sure nothing was missing, then curled up around everything she owned, determined to sleep with one eye open.

Scarlet woke from her midday nap rejuvenated and ready to talk to Jem. His tree house plan was really the only good one they had, so she knew she'd better encourage it and help it progress. She stood, picked a few blades of grass from her hair, and looked around. About half of the Lost Souls were gathered around the pool as if waiting for something. Scarlet headed over.

"What's up?"

"It's Smitty," said Sam. "He's got something important to show us."

Scarlet crossed her arms over her chest. "Oh really?" She knew she'd been neglecting her crew a little lately, running after anxious wildlife, but she hadn't expected them to start sharing important information without her.

Tim waved his arms and cleared his throat. "Attention,

everyone," he called. "Smitty here is about to introduce you to the key to our survival here on Island X."

The key to survival on Island X! And no one had even bothered to wake her! Scarlet's cheeks burned.

"Allow me to present the great island warrior . . . ahem . . . Runs with Daggers . . . and his faithful sidekick . . . Butternut!"

"What?" said Scarlet.

"Who?" said Sam.

Smitty pranced into their midst. A grass skirt hung from his waist, and two enormous leaves covered his arms like wings. His entire body still had a faint violet hue, and he'd painted his face with purple stripes and polka dots. He brandished a club at the spectators. A few Lost Souls gasped. A few more guffawed.

"I'm the fearless island warrior, Runs with Daggers!" Smitty cried. "And this is my sidekick, Butternut." He looked around. "Hey! Where is he?"

There was a rustle behind a nearby tree, and Liam reluctantly stepped out. He was dressed in a similar costume, but wore half a hollowed-out squash on his head. Judging by the dark look on his freckled face, the uniform had not been his idea.

The Lost Souls stared for a moment, openmouthed, before bursting into laughter.

"Laugh all you want," said Smitty, "but I'm on to something. If we want to scare away the pirates, we have to take advantage of what the island has to offer. Like the Islanders did back when they lived here."

"You think they wore squash helmets?" Tim howled.

"Maybe if they wanted their enemies to die laughing!" Monty called out.

Liam lifted his headpiece and tossed it on the ground. "I told you the hat wouldn't work," he said to Smitty, who dove for it, dusted it off, and plopped it back on Liam's head.

"You'll thank me in battle."

"What's with your names?" asked Elmo. "Why Runs with Daggers and . . ." He grinned. "Butternut?"

"They're intimidating," said Smitty. "Well, Runs with Daggers is, anyway. Butternut pays a nice tribute to the island resources." Just then he caught sight of Scarlet in the crowd. "Cap'n!" he cried. "What do you think? Would the Islanders have approved?"

All eyes turned to Scarlet.

"Well . . ." Scarlet knew Smitty didn't mean to disrespect her ancestors. Not long ago she'd told him that they used plants for everything, even clothes. "I'm not sure they dressed up like . . . that." She waved to Liam's hat. "Maybe . . . when they wanted to be mistaken for vegetables." The Lost Souls burst into laughter. "But, Liam, where did you find that squash?"

"In the jungle." Liam took off his hat again and tossed it to Tim, who plopped it on his own head and began to dance a jig. The Lost Souls laughed harder and more of them joined in.

Scarlet watched her crew dance around Liam and Smitty, then she silently slipped away. She didn't want to ruin their fun, but she was certain that her time could be better spent working on a plan to prepare for Lucas's return with the *Dark Ranger* pirates. She headed toward Jem's usual sleeping spot.

She found him on his belly on the grass, waving his bare feet in the air and drawing on his map with a big red feather dipped in berry juice. Scarlet had yet to look at the map, still hoping that her Islander instincts would kick in and she wouldn't need to.

Upon seeing her, Jem sat up, looking serious. "I've mapped out a spot for the tree house village." He moved over so she could share the cloak underneath him. "I think we should build a few more houses along the main trail so we can post lookouts to watch for invaders."

Good old Fitz, Scarlet thought. He always had his priorities straight. No squash helmets or grass skirts for him. She sat down beside him but didn't look at the map.

He noticed right away. "Don't you want to see where the tree houses will be?"

"Oh, um . . ." Scarlet hesitated. "All right." She took a quick glance at the map, then looked away. "Looks good."

"Captain," Jem said tentatively. "Are you actually trying not to look at the map?"

"Me?" Scarlet forced a laugh, knowing that if she explained her logic, she'd only sound loony. Again. Jem was a trustworthy pirate, and she didn't want him to question her sanity. She didn't want to question that herself. "Of course not! That's silly." She avoided looking at Jem as well.

"Right. I just thought . . . hey!" Jem straightened and squinted across the clearing. "Is that—?"

"What?" Scarlet turned, relieved at the distraction.

Jem stood up. "I thought I saw something . . . Scarlet, look at your things." He pointed at her belongings, which she'd left in a neat pile. Now they were strewn about as if a tiny hurricane had blown through camp with an eye for her things alone.

"Again?" Scarlet jumped to her feet and ran to the other side of the pool with Jem close behind. When she reached the scene she stopped. Her coat, which she'd lately been using as a pillow, was gone. "Mon-keeeey!" she screeched.

"Wait." Jem shielded his eyes from the sun. "Look, over there!" He pointed to the edge of the clearing, a good thirty yards away.

Scarlet turned just in time to see a shadow duck into the trees. "Monkey, if that was you, I'm going to string you up by your tail!" she shouted.

"Monkey?" Jem said. "I think it was a person."

Scarlet shook her head. "I'm going after it."

Jem didn't hesitate. "I'll come with you."

"That's nice of you, Fitz, but it's not necessary. I can take on a monkey."

"Sure, but what if it's a pirate?" Jem replied.

Scarlet had no answer for that. She plunged into the trees with Jem fast on her heels.

CHAPTER SIX

Scarlet was sorely missing her boots. But with Jem trotting behind her in fine expensive footwear, she couldn't bear to stop and remove the slivers that pricked the soles of her feet. She bounded on, trying hard not to yelp.

She thought she'd seen the thief a few minutes before, but now she wasn't so sure. Whether monkey or pirate, it was small and light-footed and barely left a trail for them to follow.

"I think I see it!" Jem puffed behind her. "Swing right!"

Scarlet swung right, trying to scan the jungle, dodge trees, and avoid sharp objects on the ground all at once. It didn't work. The toenail on her left big toe found a twisted root and lodged into it, bending backward as she tripped and fell with a shriek.

"Scurvy! Blast! Blimey!" She sat on the jungle floor cradling her foot, which bled where the toenail had cracked. "Did we lose it?" she asked without looking up at Jem. He looked back at her with a why-on-earth-did-you-give-your-boots-to-a-monkey face.

"I don't know," he replied. "Ugh, that looks painful."

His sympathy made her feel a bit better. Scarlet struggled to her feet and limped on through the brush.

"Wait." Jem turned around in a circle. "Which way were we headed?"

Scarlet paused, suddenly unsure. Giant ferns leaned

in from all sides. Vines hung like ship's ropes overhead, and tall, towering trees shot up to the sky, blocking the sun. They were in the depths of the jungle, and Scarlet couldn't tell which way the thief had gone, much less which way would take them back to camp. She remembered the stories Scary Mary used to tell her of people who'd stepped into the jungle, lured by the voices of the dead. The stories always ended the same—the people instantly lost their way and eventually their minds as they wandered aimlessly in the jungle for the rest of their lives. Scarlet had found them terrifying, every one.

"Did you . . . bring your map?" she asked, cringing as she said it.

Jem shook his head. "It's back at camp."

Scurvy, Scarlet thought. "I say we go that way." She pointed right.

"Uh . . . I don't know, Captain. I think we were headed that way." Jem pointed left.

She hated when he did that.

They looked around for a moment, then stuck out their fists and shook them three times before shooting.

Jem's paper lost to Scarlet's scissors.

"Blast. Best two out of three?" he said.

She shook her head, triumphant. "Come on. I have a good feeling about this way."

But after a half hour of twisting around trees and ducking under vines, Scarlet's good feeling had completely disappeared. Still, she pressed on with Jem at her heels, dodging giant ferns, climbing over rocks, and skirting bushes erupting with sweet-smelling flowers.

Suddenly the tree canopy opened up, the jungle curtains parted, and the pair found themselves in a clearing. Scarlet was about to cheer when she realized that this wasn't, in fact, the clearing they called home. This one was smaller and didn't have the tranquil feeling that made the other so special. A skinny stream cut through the middle of it, and big azure-blue butterflies flitted around.

"Where are we?" she asked.

Jem looked around. "I have no idea."

Scarlet stepped toward the blue butterflies, but they scattered the moment her shadow fell over them. "Well, I guess I'll clean this in the stream while we're here." She waved her bloody toe at Jem, who grimaced. They sat down in the shade of a giant shrub covered in purple, trumpet-shaped flowers. Scarlet swished her toe in the stream and scowled as the water stung the open wound. The butterflies settled farther downstream.

Scarlet closed her eyes, enjoying the cool shade. "Maybe it's a sign," she mused. "Maybe the island is sending us where it thinks we need to be." *There*, she thought. *That put a positive spin on being utterly lost.*

"Maybe it is a sign," Jem agreed. "A sign that we both need a map."

Scarlet opened her eyes, ready with a hot retort, but saw that he was smirking. He knew she was too proud to look at a map of Island X. She kicked up her foot and splashed him.

For a second Jem looked stunned. Then he laughed and splashed her back. "Admit it, Captain," he teased, "you need a map!"

Scarlet soaked him thoroughly. "Map *shmap*! I don't need that old thing!"

"Don't knock my map! It's—"

"Shhh." Scarlet suddenly froze and cocked her head. She motioned for Jem to stop splashing. "Did you hear that?"

He shook his head, shedding water droplets that sparkled in the sun. "What?"

She could have sworn she'd heard voices. Spirits, animals, humans—she wasn't sure. She listened again.

"He said what?"

Scarlet and Jem exchanged a wide-eyed look, then peeked around the giant shrub just in time to see three disheveled-looking pirates enter the clearing. Captain Wallace was in front, followed by Iron "Pete" Morgan and Lucas Lawrence, who were jostling for the spot immediately behind him.

"He said a bird dropped the ruby," Lucas said as he elbowed Pete in the ribs. "One of those red aras, 'parently."

Scarlet put her finger to her lips and pointed at the shrub. Making as little noise as possible, she flattened herself on the grass and slithered under its branches, then shimmied her way inside it. Jem followed. Soon both were huddled inside the shrub, peering out at the scene between droopy purple flowers.

"That," said Pete, "is complete bilge, boy. Little Harry's been into the grog again. You haven't been around long enough to know whose stories to trust." He shoulder-checked Lucas out of the way. "Isn't that right, Captain?"

The captain turned suddenly, and his crewmen stopped shoving each other. "A ruby, you say?" His upper lip twitched hungrily.

"Uh-huh," Lucas said. "Harry said it nearly fell on his head. Said he followed the bird for a while but lost it. That's why he broke away from the crew when we were hiking back this morning."

Scarlet and Jem looked at each other, wide-eyed. A pirate had actually witnessed an ara drop a ruby! Silently, Scarlet cursed her favorite birds. Why couldn't they keep a handle on their gems?

"Bilge," Pete scoffed. "Harry stepped off the trail to get into the grog. This is his excuse for not sharing."

"I believe him," Lucas insisted.

The nerve Lucas had, challenging Captain Wallace's right-hand man! Scarlet wondered why Pete hadn't strung him upside down from the main mast by now. Maybe, she reasoned, he was planning to use Lucas as smelly wild pig bait. That would certainly make her life easier.

Now the pirates were standing right beside the shrub. Captain Wallace reached out and absently plucked a purple bloom. He went to tuck it behind his ear, then slipped it in his pocket instead. "Maybe we should set up camp here," he said. "It's not as dark as the spot you chose, Pete. And I'll bet there aren't as many spiders."

"Then tell me, gullible child," Pete said, ignoring his captain, "have you ever seen a ruby fall from the sky?"

"No." Lucas crossed his big arms.

"And does Mad Little Harry actually have the treasure to prove it?"

"Well . . . no. He said he dropped it running after the bird."

Pete laughed. "Of course he did. See, Captain—"

"He what?" Captain Wallace shrieked. "He lost a ruby in the jungle? Why, that lout. That pitiful excuse for a pirate. Make him swab the deck for a year, Pete. No! Better yet, have him keelhauled!"

"Keelhauled?" Pete repeated. He hesitated a moment, as if debating whether the punishment really fit the crime.

"Too soft, are you? Fine then. Lucas, have Harry keelhauled," the captain commanded.

"Done, Cap'n." Lucas grinned, showing all his yellow teeth. The sight of them made Scarlet cringe. She resolved to brush her own teeth at least once a week.

"Good. Now let's talk rubies." Captain Wallace licked his lips. "They're my favorite jewels, you know."

"Mine too, Cap'n," Lucas said.

Inside the shrub, Scarlet and Jem rolled their eyes at each other. Outside, Pete balled his hands into fists and pierced Lucas with a broadsword glare.

"Can I see the map, Cap'n?" Lucas asked. Captain Wallace pulled a scroll out of his coat. It was the map that Uncle Finn himself had drawn years ago.

Jem growled softly. "Thief," he whispered.

"We're right about here." Lucas jabbed at a spot on the map. "Not far from the treasure, which must be where the Lost Souls are camped. When we ambush 'em, we'll come from this side"—he pointed again—"away from the trail they'll expect us to take." He turned away from Pete, who had to crane his neck to see the map.

"Excellent," Captain Wallace said. His lip twitched again. "We'll attack them when they least expect it with our strongest men out front to slay those disgusting pigs."

Scarlet looked at Jem. She didn't like where this was going. Nor did she like how close the pirates were to their very noses. In fact, Pete looked like he was about to lean right on the shrub. And if he did . . .

Jem jabbed Scarlet in the ribs to get her attention, then tilted his head to the left. Following his cue, Scarlet looked and saw two more men march into the clearing.

More pirates! Scarlet wondered where they were all camped. Then she squinted at them between the leaves. These pirates looked strangely well dressed. And they walked with more of a clip than a swagger. And they—

Scarlet dug her fingernails into Jem's arm, and he turned to her, slack-jawed.

"The King's Men!" they mouthed in unison.

"But how?" Scarlet mouthed.

Jem just shrugged.

The King's Men had halted and were staring at the pirates, who had yet to notice them. Lucas was crouched by the stream for a drink of water, and Pete stood behind him as if debating whether to push him in.

"You think the treasure might be rubies, Lucas?" Captain Wallace's lip was twitching uncontrollably. He plucked another flower off the shrub.

"Seems like it." Lucas dipped his hand in the water and slurped from it.

"Bah. Just because of some—" Pete began.

"It does, doesn't it?" said the captain. "Can you

imagine?" He dropped his flower and grabbed a fistful of blooms.

"I sure can! We'll be rich!" Lucas slapped the water, splashing the blue butterflies and sending them fluttering off in a huff.

"A great big mound of rubies!" Captain Wallace tossed the crumpled flowers in the air and spun around. "There for the taking! It's—"

Suddenly the captain's eyes fell on the strangers, and he froze, arms outstretched. Lucas looked up from the water, and Pete looked up from Lucas. All three stared across the clearing at the King's Men. Then they looked at each other. Then back at the King's Men. Captain Wallace slowly lowered his arms.

For a few moments the men in blue didn't move. Scarlet took deep breaths to slow her whomping heart and the voice in her head—her own this time—screaming, "How did they get here? What does this mean?"

Slowly, the King's Men began to move closer. One raised a hand to the pirates, who looked at one another and shrugged. Captain Wallace waved back.

"Hullo!" one of the King's Men called.

"Halloo!" Captain Wallace replied.

The King's Men stopped a few yards away from the pirates. No one seemed to be able to think of anything to say.

"This is so awkward," Jem whispered.

But Scarlet was barely watching the exchange; her eyes were glued on the newcomers. From their shoulders down they looked like twins, with identical blue trousers and identical coats with brass buttons. The one farther away had more little medals hanging over his heart and golden tassels on his shoulders—clearly higher in rank than the other. Their faces were different, though. The one nearer to the shrub had pasty, pockmarked skin and brownish-green eyes. The one farther away had a more stern face, with a sharp jaw and eyes the color of the sea after a storm.

Scarlet gasped, then slapped her hand over her mouth.

Outside the shrub, the pirates and King's Men all paused at the sound and looked around. Seeing nothing, they resumed staring awkwardly at one another.

Jem looked at Scarlet quizzically. "What?" he mouthed.

She shook her head, squeezed her eyes shut, and then looked out on the scene again.

Nothing had changed. The *Dark Ranger* pirates still faced the King's Men.

And the King's Man farthest from her was still Admiral John McCray.

Scarlet's father.

CHAPTER SEVEN

Jem wondered if Scarlet might be sick. She'd looked rather green since they'd witnessed the pirates meeting the King's Men. Not that he blamed her. Having the pirates on Island X with clues about the treasure was bad enough. Throw in some blue and brass, and there was real trouble. Now they had to fend off two groups of much larger, much stronger enemies.

But still, he hadn't expected her to react the way she did, all flustered and unable to concentrate. After their long run home (made longer by the fact that he'd steered them in the wrong direction—twice), Jem had to remind her to tell the others about this new danger. She'd been ready to go sit with the aras all evening.

"Right. Good call, Fitz." Scarlet looked sheepish. "Could you round up the crew? Let them know it's important."

Thinking that "important" was the understatement of the century, Jem jogged off, shaking his head.

"The *who*?" Ronagh screeched at the news.

"King's Men *and* pirates?" Emmett paled.

"Double trouble," Smitty moaned.

"What're the King's Men doing here?" asked Gil.

Scarlet raised her hands, palms up. "Who knows? Maybe they've pillaged all the other islands and now have to face the ones that always scared them off."

"D'ya think they know about the treasure?" Liam asked.

"They do now," said Jem. "One of the pirates saw an ara drop a ruby today, and those stupid swabs were hollering about it when the King's Men came into the clearing."

"Triple trouble," Smitty groaned.

"What're we going to do now?" asked Edwin.

All heads turned back to Scarlet, who was staring at the trees, lost in thought. When she noticed their eyes on her, she shook her head and cleared her throat. "Right. Yes. I agree."

"With what, Cap'n?" asked Tim.

Scarlet seemed distraught. "Look . . . I need time to think. Right now there's something . . ." She rubbed her temples. "Maybe an ant colony this time?"

"Ant colony?" Tim said, looking bewildered.

"I've got to go." Scarlet stood. "But I want everyone to think hard about this. We've got to make a plan." She turned away, then turned back. "Oh, and let's take turns on night watch. Just in case." Then she hurried off into the trees.

"Ant colony?" Tim repeated.

"What are we going to do?" asked Monty.

"How can we face the pirates *and* the King's Men?" Sam sniffed. The others shrugged and whispered nervously to one another.

Jem was about to remind them that worrying wouldn't help matters, and that they'd be better off doing something useful, like building tree houses, when Ronagh spoke up.

"Wait, everyone. We've still got the animals on our side, remember?"

"Of course!" Elmo exclaimed.

"They'll save us!" other Lost Souls chimed in, looking relieved.

"But what if the pigs aren't around when the pirates or King's Men invade?" Jem had to ask. "Or what if they decide not to help? I think we should have a backup plan. Like the tree—"

"Then we'll make sure that they stay on our side," Ronagh interjected. She thought for a moment, then announced, "I've got an idea." And she marched off across the clearing.

"I've got one, too," said Smitty. "C'mon, Liam."

"Things were just so much easier back on the *Hop*, weren't they?" said Tim. "I'm going to check up on her from the cliff. Anyone want to come?" A few Lost Souls nodded and followed him.

"Wait!" Jem called. "We need to work on a plan together. We . . ."

But everyone was already walking away, leaving Jem to wonder what on earth was *wrong* with these pirates.

Jem assessed the situation during his night-watch shift after he'd wandered around the clearing a few times with a jar of fireflies to light his way.

The crew was feeling very lost—that much was clear. A few weeks ago, they'd have been delighted to take on the pirates and King's Men simultaneously. But here on

Island X they didn't know what to do or where to put their efforts. They needed someone to direct them.

Jem sat down on the grass and tapped on the jar to keep the fireflies awake. The problem was, the Lost Souls' leader wasn't being her usual take-charge self. Not that Jem blamed her. Scarlet certainly had a lot on her mind—and a lot going on inside it, apparently. But still, the Lost Souls needed a leader.

"I'd do it myself if they ever listened to me," he told the fireflies. "But I can't even get the Housing Committee to do its job." The insects' lights flickered, then disappeared altogether. Jem sighed and released them into the night. He tucked his hands inside his coat sleeves and drew his knees to his chin to keep warm.

As the sky began to lighten in the east, he concluded that the best thing he could do was build the tree houses himself. If he couldn't get the others to help, at least he could do his part.

Most of the Lost Souls were still curled up on the grass, snoring or muttering in their sleep, while Jem got to work. He consulted his map and headed for the spot he'd chosen for the first house—a cluster of sturdy trees close to the mouth of the trail, yet far enough away from the aras so as not to disturb or draw attention to them.

First, he decided, he had to gather wood. Thankfully there was no shortage of that. He collected some building supplies that Tim had hauled up from the *Hop*—a hammer, nails, and rope—and headed off toward the trees.

On the other side of the clearing, Jem saw Scarlet

wandering with her hands in her trouser pockets, looking as if she hadn't slept at all. He considered running over to check up on her but decided against it. When Captain McCray was lacking sleep, the smallest slip of the tongue could see a pirate cleaning the long drop for a week.

Hoping she hadn't spotted him, Jem slipped into the jungle.

His construction plan was fairly simple: He'd collect bundles of long sticks and tie them together side by side to form a platform. Then he'd balance the platform between the branches of four trees to make the floor of the house. In that same fashion, he'd build the walls and even the roof and cover the house with big, flat leaves. He imagined the Lost Souls huddling around firefly lanterns at night in their little tree houses, listening to the rain on their leafy roofs and praising Jem's clever architectural skills. Oh, they'd thank him, all right.

He didn't have to look far to find long sticks lying on the jungle floor. He stooped and collected until he had a good-size bundle, and he was just about to move it when Ronagh appeared holding a feather, a jar of crushed berries, and a piece of bark like the one he'd used to make his map.

"I need your help," she announced.

Jem doubted it had anything to do with tree houses. But he dropped the bundle and wiped his forehead. "What's up?" He looked more closely at her supplies. "Hey, is that my quill and ink?"

Ronagh nodded. "I borrowed them." She held up the bark. "I need you to write something for me."

"Write something? Now?" Jem looked down at his bundle and then back at Ronagh.

"It's important. It'll help protect Island X."

Jem sighed. At least she was trying. "All right." He took the quill and bark and sat down with Ronagh beside him. "What do you want me to write?"

"A letter. To the smelly wild pigs."

"A letter to . . ." Jem arched an eyebrow. "Ro, I'm not sure they can read."

She looked impatient. "It doesn't matter. We'll put it in writing, and everyone will sign. It'll be sym . . . symbol . . ."

"Symbolic," Jem finished for her.

"Right," she said firmly, and Jem decided it would be faster not to argue.

"All right. Dictate away."

"What does that mean?"

"Just tell me what to write."

Ronagh cleared her throat. "Dear Pigs. We, the Lost Souls of Island X, are honored to live beside you in this clearing. We like you very much and don't even mind your smell."

Jem looked up. "Really?"

Ronagh nodded. He dipped his quill in the ink and scribbled the message.

"We promise never to harm you or eat you, and we'll protect you from anyone who would."

Jem scribbled faster.

"You have our word. Love, the Lost Souls. There, do you think they'll like it?" she asked anxiously.

Jem finished writing with a flourish. "How could they not?"

"That's what I thought. Now sign here." She pointed, and Jem obeyed. Satisfied, Ronagh wandered off to collect more signatures.

Shaking his head, Jem returned to his task. He decided that the best way to move his pile of sticks would be to tie them up. He grabbed the rope he'd brought and fished in his pocket for his knife.

Only his pocket was empty.

"Hey!" he cried. "Where is it?" He pulled his pocket inside out and watched some lint flutter to the ground. "But how . . . ?" He always kept his knife in his pocket. The only time it wasn't there was when he was using it. Well, except for the time that Gil and Lucas stole it . . .

The thought made him pause. He suddenly remembered Edwin's missing dagger. Perhaps Gil was up to his old tricks.

But before he could ponder that further, he caught sight of a familiar egg-shaped figure on the path nearby.

"Uncle Finn!" Jem practically leaped with joy, forgetting all about his knife. "Where *were* you?" He crashed through the trees toward his uncle. Thomas towered behind Uncle Finn, looking around as if taking in the place for the first time.

"Jem, my boy!" Uncle Finn cried as Jem leaped onto the path in front of them.

"I'm so glad you're here. I tried to call you, but it didn't work," he panted, leaning over to catch his breath. "This pipe thing. It was faulty."

Uncle Finn looked confused. "The what? Stand up, boy. Talk slowly. We've had very little sleep lately and Thomas . . . well, I'll explain about Thomas later."

Jem looked at the giant, who'd scooped a fuzzy brown spider off the ground and was inspecting it like it was the most intriguing thing he'd ever seen. The spider curled into a ball on Thomas's palm, obviously terrified. Jem looked back at Uncle Finn, who only shook his head. "Later."

"Right. Well, it didn't work, Uncle Finn. The pipe you gave me. I tried to call you when the pirates invaded, but that noisemaker seriously scuttles—didn't make a sound. Maybe you—"

"Pirates? Invaded? Stop babbling, boy, and tell me exactly what happened."

Jem took a deep breath and began his tale from the beginning.

"Oh, and the King's Men are here now, too," he concluded. "Scarlet and I saw them while hiding in a shrub yesterday."

Uncle Finn looked as though he were seasick. "I have to sit down." He found a boulder and sank down onto it, mopping his face with his handkerchief. "All right. So you don't know where the *Dark Ranger* pirates are camped now?"

"*Dark Ranger*?" Thomas stopped poking the spider, which promptly leaped off his hand and rappelled to the ground on a strand of silk. "That's a funny name. Finn, have I heard of the *Dark Ranger*?"

Jem looked from his uncle to Thomas and back to his uncle. "What's with him?"

"Oh, just an experiment gone slightly awry." Uncle Finn dismissed it with a wave of his handkerchief.

"What? What did you do to Thomas?"

"I didn't *do* anything to him, Jem," Finn snapped. "He'll be himself in no time. Anyway, it was a great step forward in our study. We disproved our hypothesis that *Bediotropicanus onicus* cures androgenetic alopecia. Rather, it swiftly erases one's memory. Thankfully, Thomas ingested only a small amount."

Jem's mouth fell open.

"Oh, don't worry, nephew. He'll be right as rain tomorrow, ready to work again. We're making great progress. Our first sample, *Bediotropicanus plumpicus*, turned Thomas's hair a gorgeous shade of green—made him blend right into the trees. Look, you might still be able to see it." He motioned for Thomas to turn around, and the giant obeyed. On the back of his head, his brown hair was streaked with emerald green.

"Wow," said Jem.

"Impressive, isn't it?" Uncle Finn patted Thomas on the back. "So we've eliminated two *Bedio*s, and I've come to the exciting conclusion that the one we want is so close it's practically in this clearing. Which is fortunate, because with the pirates and King's Men on the island, I won't be leaving you children alone."

"The King's Men," Thomas said thoughtfully, turning back around. "They sound nice."

"It'll all come back to him, Jem. Don't look so worried." Uncle Finn yawned. "Now I, for one, am going to take a nap."

"Wait." Jem dug in his pocket and pulled out the noisemaker. "Can you look at this first?"

Uncle Finn took the noisemaker, motioned for Jem and Thomas to cover their ears, then blew into it with all his might. Nothing happened.

"*Hmph*," he grunted. "I could've sworn . . ." He held the pipe up to his eye and squinted into it. "Aha." Raising an eyebrow at Jem, he tapped the pipe against the palm of his other hand. Out slid a small blue-and-black-striped worm. It looked at them with a dazed expression similar to Thomas's, then rolled into a ball.

"Oh," said Jem. "Oops."

"Indeed." Uncle Finn handed him the pipe and placed the worm on a nearby leaf. "Not faulty. Just occupied." He yawned again. "Now for that nap. Really, you have no idea how exhausting it is making groundbreaking discoveries."

CHAPTER EIGHT

"Jem. Jem, wake up."

"Mmph?" Jem rolled over, pulling himself out of a dream in which Ronagh had dressed the wild pigs in matching squash bonnets.

"I need your help," Uncle Finn said.

"Again?" Jem murmured, turning away. "I'm not writing another letter to the pigs."

"What are you talking about? Wake up." Uncle Finn gave him a firm thump on the shoulder.

Jem blinked, trying to focus on his uncle in the early-morning light. A light mist had settled on the clearing, and Uncle Finn's bald head was covered in tiny water droplets.

"I want to start cataloging the specimens," Uncle Finn said, "and Thomas is still a bit muddled. He won't be much help, but you know the process."

"Erghm." Jem blinked away an image of the pigs in squash bonnets and sat up.

"Excellent. It'll only take a few hours."

Jem rubbed his gritty eyes. The dew had seeped through his cloak and into his trousers. He grimaced. Oh, for a tree house, high and dry. This was no time to be cataloging bromeliads.

He found Uncle Finn near the pool, gobbling handfuls of nuts while studying the plant cuttings he'd spread out on a spare black cloak.

"I don't know how you children survive on this diet," Uncle Finn grumbled, spewing crumbs. "I am ravenous. Last night I merely suggested we catch a wild boar for dinner, and I was assailed by a small but ferocious . . . *vegetarian*." He harrumphed. "Honestly. Who doesn't eat meat?"

"Think it's a nice idea, m'self." Jem and Uncle Finn turned to see Thomas approaching them a little unsteadily. "The animals round here are nice. Specially the pigs, though, they do smell somethin' nasty."

Jem nodded and smiled at the giant. "Feeling better, Thomas?"

Thomas nodded. "The green in my hair's nearly gone. I'm just havin' a hard time rememberin' some things. Specially names."

"Well, I'm Jem. Finn's nephew."

"Jem. Nephew." Thomas nodded as if storing the information away.

Uncle Finn harrumphed again. "Personally, I think the pigs would be nicer alongside mashed potatoes. Oh, don't look at me like that. I won't harm your porcine partners. But I think this diet has affected your brains." He stood and wiped crumbs off his beard. "You do know that all these wild pigs came from the Old World, don't you?"

"Really?" asked Thomas.

"Of course. The first Old Worlders to set foot on these islands shipped over scores of domesticated pigs and set them free. And *why* do you think they did that?"

"For company?" Thomas suggested.

"For FOOD!" Uncle Finn yelled. Then he sighed and wiped his head with his sleeve.

"Why don't I go find us some fruit to go with those nuts?" Jem offered, and he slipped away before Uncle Finn could object. He was certain Thomas would insist on helping catalog, which would leave him free to work on the tree houses.

He hadn't gone far when he came upon a group of Lost Souls sitting on the damp ground, and he had only a moment to wonder what they were up to before a voice cut through the mist.

"Attention all Lost Souls!" the voice announced. "Feast your eyes on the latest and greatest island warrior and his trusty sidekick!"

Smitty stepped out from behind a misty curtain, shouting into a big rolled-up leaf. This time he wore a massive headpiece made of green parrot feathers, and he'd again decorated his face in purple stripes and polka dots. On his bare chest he'd drawn a bird. Smitty placed his hands on his hips and puffed out his chest so they could all admire his artwork.

Liam stepped out, too, looking not nearly as proud of his ensemble. And no wonder, because while Smitty had dressed himself like a bird, he'd chosen a seashore theme for Liam. The younger boy wore a seaweed headscarf and matching skirt.

Smitty wiggled his eyebrows, cleared his throat, and burst into song:

*Prepare to be astounded at my greatest costume
    yet.*

*And not to worry, Ronagh: No birds were
    harmed for it.*

*I found these jolly feathers underneath a molting
    bird*

*who didn't seem to mind—in fact, I think he
    was flattered.*

*At any rate, that bird inspired a brand-new
    uniform.*

As soon as I slipped into it, I felt myself transform

into an island warrior—a mighty one with heft.

*What else could I be called except the Deadly
    Parrot of Death?*

"The Deadly Parrot of Death?" Monty echoed.

"That's rather repetitive," Tim commented.

"Shhh," Smitty said. He continued.

But don't forget my sidekick, a child of the sea.

*He may lack my charisma, and he does smell
    like algae.*

*And yet the faithful Crab Cake has some talents
    of his own.*

*Run for your life if you should see him reaching
    for a stone.*

On cue, Liam held up a pebble. "There is one good thing about this costume." He pulled out a slingshot made of seaweed and driftwood, then loaded the pebble into its clamshell pocket and let it fly, just above the Lost Souls' heads. The crowd's laughter turned to *ooh*s of admiration.

"Nice slingshot, Liam!"

"Now that's a good way to fight off those scalawags!"

"Ah, but look what I've got!" Smitty cried, not to be outdone. He produced a bow of sorts, made with a curved stick and some thin rope. Then he took a stick that he'd whittled to a point at one end, fitted it into the bow, and let it fly. It sailed about three feet before nose-diving into the grass.

The Lost Souls howled.

"Nice try, Deadly Parrot!"

"Give it to me! I bet I can do it!"

Jem chose that moment to slip away. Costumes and new weapons were all fine and good, but he had tree houses to build. He'd wasted enough time already. With pirates and King's Men on the island, he had to get to work.

"Today I'll finish the floor and start on the walls," he muttered to himself, hurrying into the trees, "which shouldn't be—*oof!*" Jem ran smack into someone hurrying out of the trees and tumbled backward into a shrub with very prickly leaves. "Argh!" He rolled to the side, trying to see who or what he'd collided with.

Gil lay in a pile of leaves a few feet away, rubbing his elbow. For a moment he looked dangerously close to throwing a temper tantrum, then seemed to change his mind.

"You all right, mate?"

"Fine," Jem grumbled, although he felt as if a hundred tiny ants had marched up his shirt to sting his neck and shoulders.

"Sorry 'bout that, Fitz. Didn't see you coming." Gil stood and offered Jem a filthy hand up.

Jem grunted and picked himself up without Gil's help. "What are you doing?"

"Me?" Gil looked away. "Nothing."

"Nothing?"

"Not really." He brushed off his dirty shirt without looking at Jem.

"You were in the jungle at daybreak doing nothing?" Jem asked, immediately suspicious.

Gil sniffed. "If you have to know, I was . . . you know. Doing my business."

"Oh." Jem couldn't say much to that.

"That's right. And what about you?"

"I'm going to build tree houses."

"Huh. Well, good luck with that." Gil slipped past him, headed toward the clearing.

"Wait, Gil, one second." Jem couldn't help but ask. "Have you . . . have you seen my pocketknife lately?"

Gil stopped and looked back. "No. Why?"

"Because it's missing. And I . . . well, I just . . ." Jem trailed off. He really had no good reason to accuse Gil of stealing it. Except that, the last time it had gone missing . . .

"Thought I stole it?" Gil snapped. "Oh, that's nice. You didn't think that maybe you just lost it. Or that someone or something else might have taken it. Nope, you just blamed it on me."

"Well, you *did* do it before," Jem mumbled.

"Well, I didn't do it this time!" Gil shouted and stomped off.

Jem watched him go. *I probably shouldn't have said anything*, he thought. *Now he'll be awful to deal with.*

He shook his head. "Focus now. The tree houses are what matter most. I've got to—"

A rustling noise in a nearby fern made him freeze. "Gil?" he called, even though he knew Gil had stomped off in the opposite direction.

The rustling stopped.

Jem inched toward the fern, hoping that by some miracle it was indeed Gil trying to scare him. Or if not Gil, something harmless. Like an iguana. A friendly, toothless one.

He paused and took a deep breath. Then he swept the fern leaves to one side just in time to see a large figure disappearing into the bushes behind it. A figure dressed in torn trousers and an old shirt.

Without a doubt, a pirate.

CHAPTER NINE

This time when Scarlet tromped through the jungle, she barely gave her bootless feet a thought. This time she had something far more important on her mind.

Jem's pirate sighting that morning had chased away all her other worries. The thought of a *Dark Ranger* dog so close to the clearing jolted her into action. There was no sense in sitting around planning for when they got attacked. It was time for offensive action. It was time for . . .

Operation Island Espionage.

Thankfully, the Lost Souls had agreed. In fact, everyone had clamored to take part in this mission, which would involve sneaking through the jungle to find out where the pirates and King's Men were camped—something they should have done immediately. There was no time to lose.

Jem, Tim, Liam, and Edwin now marched behind her, looking more determined than she'd seen them in weeks. Tim hadn't even mentioned his beloved *Hop* since Scarlet had announced this mission. She glanced over her shoulder and nodded, satisfied. This was how things ought to be. The Lost Souls didn't wait to get attacked, no, sir.

Scarlet had chosen her spies wisely, selecting only those she knew wouldn't mind splitting up to investigate on their own. For there was another part to this mission that she hadn't told them about—and *couldn't* tell them about. She needed time to herself so she could see her father again.

She wasn't exactly sure why she wanted to see the admiral. She still hadn't forgiven him for abandoning her with Scary Mary. And yet, for some strange reason, she simply had to see him. Even if just from afar.

Jem had brought along his map and was calling out directions, trying to steer them toward the clearing where he and Scarlet had seen the pirates and King's Men. He claimed he was certain that they were headed the right way, but Scarlet wasn't so sure. Above her, the afternoon sun trickled through the forest canopy, speckling the jungle floor with gold. A cicada chorus whined. A few aras flapped by, trailed by a cloud of black-and-white checkered butterflies. But nothing looked familiar to her.

Nothing, that is, until the big toe on her left foot lodged once again into a twisted root and sent her sprawling. Scarlet had just begun to hurl the worst pirate curses she knew when she recognized the root. "You scuttling scourge of the—hey! Hurray!"

Tim peered down at her over his spectacles. "Hurray? Cap'n, your toe's bleeding like a fountain. Here." He reached into his pocket and pulled out a dark blue handkerchief.

"I know! What luck!" Scarlet cried, wrapping the cloth around her poor toe, injured twice in three days. "This is the root I tripped on last time we were here. That means we're on the right track!"

"It also means you should be wearing boots," Edwin quipped. Scarlet tossed him a cutlass glare.

"See," Jem said proudly. "This is a very accurate map."

"I think I've been here before, too," said Liam. "That's where Smitty and I found the squash he made me wear." He pointed off to the right.

"I didn't know squash grew in the jungle," said Tim.

"Maybe the Islanders grew them," Liam suggested.

"Maybe." They both turned to Scarlet for an answer, and she shrugged. Vegetables weren't high on her list of things she wanted to recall.

"Right, then," said Jem. "I'll add the squash to the map. And the tripping root, too. Maybe that way you'll avoid it next time." Scarlet shot another cutlass glare, this time in his direction. He grinned and offered her a hand up.

"Well, at least we know where we are." She stood and dusted off her trousers, then continued on, trying to ignore the gigantic blue bandage on her foot.

They reached the other clearing in surprisingly little time. The blue butterflies still lazed around the stream running through it. "All right, spies," Scarlet said, "gather round. This is the place. Those swabs must be camped close by, and wherever they are, the King's Men can't be far. Let's each pick a corner of this clearing and explore the jungle beyond it. Go quietly and don't forget which way you came. We can't have anyone getting lost and stumbling into enemy territory."

Scarlet stuck her fist into the center of their huddle. The Lost Souls piled theirs on top.

"No prey, no pay, mateys."

"No prey, no pay!" they whispered, excited to hear the old chorus.

"And may you die peacefully in your sleep rather than at the paws of that mousy Captain Wallace."

"Die peacefully!"

"I'll take that corner over there. Meet back here in . . ." Scarlet paused. Timing was difficult now that there wasn't a clock to be found. "A while."

The Lost Souls scattered across the clearing. Scarlet headed for her corner, hoping that the island would steer her toward the King's Men. On her way, she detoured past the shrub in which she and Jem had hidden and grabbed a fistful of its purple flowers. She placed one on the ground as she slipped into the trees, hoping it would still be there when she needed to find her way back.

The going was slow. This part of the jungle was even thicker than the one they'd just passed through. Scarlet dropped another flower and pushed her way through.

As she shuffled along under the whining cicadas, she wondered exactly what she'd do if she did see her father. Would she hang back and spy on him? Or pop right out and say hello? No, she couldn't do that, not after all this time. What would she say, anyway? "Well now, Father, fancy meeting you in the depths of the jungle on the island of my birth. Long time no see!"

And would she even *want* to talk to him? He had, after all—

Swish.

Scarlet paused, wondering if she'd imagined that—

Swish. Swoosh.

Fortunately, there was no shortage of hiding spots. Scarlet chose a tree whose giant roots lay above the ground, almost as high as her waist. She crouched behind one of the roots and peeked over the top just in time to see a man in a blue coat walk by swinging a machete. *Swish. Swoosh.* Ferns and vines fell around him as he slashed a trail through the jungle. Scarlet cringed. She had yet to feel the distress of any island plants, but she imagined they weren't pleased at getting hacked up. The Lost Souls had long ago put away their machetes and let the island vegetation grow wherever it wanted to.

The King's Man stopped and wiped his forehead with his sleeve. He might have been twenty, but his wispy blond hair and chubby face reminded Scarlet of a toddler. Once he'd passed, she slipped out from her hiding spot and followed him.

He took quick, nervous steps as if he couldn't wait to get out of the jungle and back to his tent. A snake's tail disappearing into a pile of leaves made him yelp. A vine tickling his neck made him swing his weapon wildly. Scarlet kept back a safe distance, fairly certain this yellow-belly would lead her right where she wanted to go.

Sure enough, within minutes Scarlet found herself on the edge of yet another clearing, this one filled with gray canvas tents and men dressed in blue. Three King's Men studied a compass while two others chopped wood. Porridge bubbled on the fire, and the yellow-belly hurried over for his share of the steaming mush.

Scarlet parted the ferns a crack, studying the scene. There was something odd about it, something she couldn't quite put her finger on. Something that made her uneasy. She thought hard until she realized that she was feeling uneasy because the animals and spirits in this area were, too.

She squeezed her eyes shut, then looked at the clearing again. And realized exactly what was wrong.

"Shivers," she breathed. "I'm home."

The King's Men had gone and set up camp right where her old village had once stood. Their canvas tents sat right where the Islanders' huts once sat. Scarlet trembled, wondering what had happened to the huts. Had the Islanders taken them down? Or had they been destroyed by weather and intruders, crumbling to nothing, leaving no trace of the village that once housed Scarlet's family and so many others?

And more importantly, what the flotsam was her father doing camped here? Surely he hadn't led his men here just to cut down trees and trample the earth with their big old boots.

Scarlet scanned the camp until she found exactly what she'd come for: Off to the left, two men sat on stumps, deep in discussion. One had pasty, pockmarked skin and meek, greenish-brown eyes. The other was her father. He looked older and even stonier than he had the previous day, with creases around his gray eyes and long lines on either side of his mouth. Though she couldn't make out what he was saying, she was fairly certain it wasn't about the nice weather they were having.

She pictured this father next to the one she used to sit with while he made canoes for the Islanders. They were so very different. The old father used to carve little stars for her to wear on a thread of twine around her neck. This father chopped the air with his hands when he spoke. The old father used to hum songs and tell jokes. This one's glare could freeze an ocean.

Suddenly he stood and stalked off, leaving the pasty-skinned man looking like a dog that had been punished for chewing his master's shoes. Ignoring another man's offer of porridge, Admiral McCray headed toward the ragged path the yellow-belly had just cut. Scarlet followed him.

He marched down the path, hands balled into fists. But after a few minutes, a strange thing happened. The admiral's shoulders suddenly slumped, and his march became a shuffle. When a droopy vine brushed his head, he barely noticed. And when a giant rhinoceros beetle buzzed in his ear, he simply flicked it away with a fingernail. The beetle took the blow right on its snout and tumbled to the ground while Admiral McCray drifted on unaware.

Scarlet paused to scoop up the insect. "You all right, beetle?" she whispered.

The beetle tottered around her palm for a moment, then took off in a loopy, off-balance flight.

Scarlet ran on tiptoes to catch up to her father, but stayed several yards behind him, congratulating herself on how quietly she could sneak through the jungle.

Maybe my Islander ways are coming back to me, she

thought. *Maybe I don't need boots after all. Or a—*

She looked up just in time to see her father bending over to pick up one of her purple flowers, mere feet away. She dug her toes into the dirt and stopped short of running smack into him. Then she took a slow step back. And another. One more . . .

Admiral McCray twisted the flower between his fingers. He looked up as if searching for the tree that had dropped it. He looked left and he looked right.

Then he turned to look behind him.

Scarlet froze. Her father froze. He blinked. And blinked again. He took a step back. His mouth opened and shut, opened and shut. Suddenly he no longer looked like a hard-hearted King's Man, but like one of the smallest Lost Souls waking up from a nightmare.

"No," he whispered. "No, you're not real."

Scarlet took a step back, too. Did he really think—

"Don't do this to me, island." His voice rose. "Don't show her to me unless she's real!" His gray eyes darted around as if looking for more ghosts.

"Father," Scarlet whispered. "Don't shout. They'll hear you."

He glared at her, then shook his fist at the trees. "I said don't do this to me—"

"Oh, stop now," Scarlet interrupted, growing impatient. "The island's not doing anything. It's me, Father. Scarlet."

Admiral McCray lowered his fist and looked at her suspiciously. "How do I know?"

Scarlet threw up her hands. "I don't know. Here.

Pinch me." She held out her arm, but he recoiled. "Oh, come on. Look here. I'm bleeding." She raised her leg so he could see the bloody blue bandage. "There. Real blood."

He stared at her toe until she lowered it. Then he opened his mouth as if to speak again, but all that came out was an odd choking noise. He bit his lip like he was about to cry.

"Oh no." Scarlet was at his side in a second, laying a hand on his arm. "Oh, Father, don't do that. It's all right."

He grabbed her shoulders, turning her to face him. Then he engulfed her in a crushing hug.

Scarlet allowed it for a few moments before tapping him on the shoulder. "Father," she gasped, "I can't breathe."

He released her, but he kept his hands on her shoulders, gray eyes wide. For an instant his frown lines softened, like a great worry had just up and left him, and Scarlet caught a glimpse of the father she used to know.

But only for an instant. Then he gripped her shoulders hard, giving her a shake. "Where have you *been*?" he shouted. "And what were you *thinking*, running away? Do you have any idea what you put me through?" He gave her shoulders another shake.

Scarlet squirmed out of his grasp, startled. "Well, I—"

"Look at you—you're filthy! What on earth are you doing here?"

She crossed her arms over her chest. "First of all, Father, what *I* put *you* through? *You* were the one who abandoned me with a witch. And, anyway, what do you think you're doing camped in our old village? Hmm?"

His face suddenly went pale. "Our what?"

"Our village. The place where I was born, where we lived with my mother and—"

"That's . . ." Admiral McCray turned to look behind him. "That's not . . ."

"You didn't recognize it?" Scarlet couldn't believe it. "How could you not? It's—" She froze. "Wait, did you hear that?"

Her father looked around. "What?"

She put a finger to her lips, then grabbed his hand and yanked him off the trail and behind a tree. They both peered out as Liam marched by. By the look on his face, Scarlet knew he, too, had found the King's Men's camp.

"Who was that?" her father whispered, incredulous.

"Liam," Scarlet answered. "One of my crew."

"Your *crew*?"

Scarlet nodded. "I've got to get back to them."

"What? You're not leaving!"

"Shhh. I'll come back. But I can't stay now."

"You're *not* leaving," the admiral commanded.

Scarlet rolled her eyes. She'd forgotten how tiresome grown-ups could be. "I am," she said firmly. "But I'll be back." She turned to go, then turned back again. "You can't tell anyone about me and my crew."

"I don't even know who your crew *is*!" he hissed.

"I have to go."

Admiral McCray reached out to stop her, but Scarlet turned and sprinted after Liam.

CHAPTER TEN

Scarlet replayed her conversation with her father at least fourteen times that day and the night that followed. It was all she could think about—especially the part where he'd claimed he didn't know he was camped on the remains of their old village. Not only had he forced her to forget her past, he'd also gone and erased his own memories. *What else had he forgotten?* she wondered. *Surely*—

"Captain?"

Scarlet pulled herself back to the present. It was the morning after Operation Island Espionage, and Jem was squinting up at her from the grass, where he sat with his quill poised over his map. Several other crew members sat with him, all eyes on Scarlet.

"Um?"

"The King's Men's camp. It was about here?" He pointed to a spot east of the skull and crossbones that represented the pirates' camp. Both he and Tim had come across the *Dark Ranger*'s camp while Scarlet was off having a McCray family reunion.

"Sure, that looks about right." She shrugged.

Jem frowned. "It's just that with cartography 'about right' isn't good enough. You have to be very accurate . . ."

"Perfect, then. It's perfect," Scarlet snapped.

Jem looked surprised. "All right, all right," he

muttered and drew a large crown on the map.

"That looks jolly," said Tim. "But what do we do now? Are we actually going to attack them?"

"Sure, why not?" Smitty piped up. "If you haven't noticed, I've become rather skilled with a bow and arrow."

Scarlet gave him a tired look. Smitty's arrow couldn't hit the broadside of the *Hop*.

"And we won't be alone!" Ronagh added. "The pigs'll help. Scarlet gave them my letter, right, Scarlet?"

"Oh. Well, um . . ." Scarlet hadn't actually gotten around to delivering the letter yet, partly because she'd had other things on her mind and partly because she didn't want to pester the pigs.

"What'd they say, anyway?" Liam asked.

"They—uh—" Scarlet stammered, then sighed. "Look, Ro, I haven't delivered it yet. But I will. I just don't know . . ." *Blimey*, she thought, *if there were a medal for Worst Leader Ever, I'd be wearing it today.*

Ronagh's face fell. "You don't think it'll work? You think it's a bad letter?" She blinked hard.

Oh no, Scarlet thought. *No tears. I can't deal with tears today.* "Your letter's jolly, Ro. I'm sure it'll work. I'm just waiting . . . for a good time."

"Uh-huh." Ronagh didn't look convinced.

"Speaking of the pigs"—Jem looked up from his map—"did you know they were actually domestic in the Old World? The King's Men brought them here not long ago."

Scarlet looked down at him. "So?"

"Well, I was thinking that maybe that's where they learned English," Jem suggested.

Liam laughed. "That's a good one, Fitz. And maybe they learned to read compasses and sail schooners, too."

Cheeks red, Jem turned back to his map. "I think it's a rather good theory."

"All right," Scarlet broke in. "I have an idea." She didn't really. She just wanted to distract Liam and Jem from an argument and Ronagh from her sniffles. "Ronagh, I'll need your help. Liam, too."

"What for?" Ronagh wiped her nose on her sleeve.

"To . . ." Scarlet paused, thinking fast. "To see if there's some way we can hide the aras." It wasn't a great mission, but it couldn't hurt.

"Okay." Ronagh shrugged, and Liam climbed to his feet.

Minutes later they were standing beneath the ara rookery, watching sparkles of red through the leaves.

"Just as I thought," said Scarlet. "They're too easy to spot. A pirate could find those rubies in the dark."

"Or a King's Man," Ronagh added. Scarlet cringed, thinking of her father.

Ronagh tapped her chin. "Maybe we can make a huge curtain with palm leaves."

Liam snorted. "We might as well put up a big sign that says 'Guess What's Behind Door Number One?'" Ronagh poked him in the stomach. "Ow!" He reached for one of her braids just as someone came crashing through the bushes behind them. They all turned to see Emmett, panting and flushed.

"A King's Man," he puffed. "Headed this way."

"Already?" Scarlet cried. "I mean, what did he look like?"

Emmett paused to think. "Um . . . he wore a blue coat?"

"Forget it. I'll go look. You warn the crew."

"We'll come with you!" said Ronagh.

Scarlet hesitated. If it was indeed the admiral, she couldn't have her friends witnessing a father-daughter exchange. But if it wasn't him, well, it would be nice to have some backup.

"All right. Which way?"

Emmett pointed, then ran for the clearing.

They tiptoed through the jungle, and with every step Scarlet grew more and more certain that the intruder was her father. She could feel his presence in her bones, just the way she used to when she lived with Scary Mary and would lie awake at night, listening for the sound of his footsteps on the stairs when he returned home for a visit.

"You two, go that way." She pointed to the left. "If you see him heading toward the aras, distract him. I'll go this way."

Ronagh and Liam headed left, and Scarlet continued on, sneaking through the bushes until she spotted him.

It was indeed Admiral McCray, looking just as sour as the day before.

"Father," Scarlet greeted him, slipping out of the trees.

He jumped, and for an instant his face brightened before he scowled again. "Scarlet," he snapped, "I don't like this one bit. I won't have my daughter living like a . . . a . . ."

"A what?" Scarlet asked. "An Islander?" He shut his mouth. "Come on. You can't be here." She led him back down the path the way he'd come.

"Why not?" he asked, jogging to keep up with her. "You're my daughter. I have a right to see how you live. And with whom."

Scarlet grunted. He certainly hadn't given a fig about how she lived after they'd left the island. Or with whom.

"Daughter." He reached for her shoulder, and she turned to face him, hands on her hips. He looked flustered, as if realizing that commanding the King's Men had nothing on commanding a twelve-year-old girl. "I must know what you've been doing these past years. You must tell me."

Scarlet swallowed and looked away. "Fine. I've been . . ." Now she had to choose her words carefully. "I've been leading a crew."

"A crew," he repeated. "A crew of . . ."

"Children."

"Children," he said. "No parents?"

"Uh-uh." Scarlet felt a tiny twinge of guilt for leaving out the crucial details. *Did that count as lying?* she wondered. *And did it even matter?* The Lost Souls' most important rule was that their identity must be kept a secret from the rest of the world. That didn't change, even if Lucas had spilled the beans to his new crew. Or if one of them was reuniting with a long-lost parent. She went on to tell him that her crew's mission was to protect Island X—skipping over the part about terrorizing the ships of both pirates and King's Men.

Then she shook her finger at him. "But you can't tell anyone."

Admiral McCray opened his mouth as if to protest, then shut it, looking put out. Finally he asked, "Are there . . . Islanders in your crew?"

Surprised, Scarlet shook her head. "Of course not."

The admiral frowned and looked at the ground.

They walked in silence for several minutes, he staring at the dirt and she at the tree canopy. Morning light was weaving through the leaves, bathing the birds and bugs in sunshine. The admiral looked up now and then to steal glances at Scarlet, but she pretended not to notice.

When he finally spoke, his voice was softer. "How long have you been living here?"

"A . . . while," Scarlet said carefully.

"And you're camped in that clearing back there?"

She nodded. Then a thought occurred to her. "Do you remember the place all the Islanders used to visit?" she asked. "It was a special place, with a certain feeling . . ."

He looked blank.

"Oh, you *must* remember it," she insisted. "The grown-ups would harvest spices, and the children would play, and there was this particular feeling . . ."

His shook his head.

"But you used to—"

"I don't remember it," the admiral interrupted firmly.

Maddening grown-up, Scarlet thought. She pressed on. "How could you forget? And while we're on the topic, how could you go and camp in our old village?"

The admiral threw his hands up. "I just forgot! I'd completely forgotten what the old village looked like until you appeared and reminded me."

Studying his face, Scarlet knew he was telling the truth. And it occurred to her that had she not worked so hard to reconnect with the island herself, she might not have recognized the village site, either. That made her even more annoyed.

"Well . . . why did you bring your men here in the first place?" she asked. "I mean, you must have known where you were going. Couldn't you have picked another island?"

"Perhaps you've forgotten, Scarlet," he said, "that I'm not ultimately in charge. I take orders, too. And I was ordered to bring the men here to scout for wood and spices and . . . whatever else we could find."

"Well," she sputtered, "couldn't you have, I don't know, steered them off course? That's what I'd—"

She stopped as an intense feeling of distress cut through her brain. Panicky, like that pesky monkey. Well, he'd just have to wait.

"I hope you're aware that there are pirates around," said the admiral.

"Oh, we know," she replied, then realized that he might have useful information. "Are your men keeping an eye on them?"

"Yes," he said. "Although I doubt they're much of

a threat to us. Not with old Captain What's-his-name in charge."

In spite of herself and the situation, Scarlet smiled. "He's a few barrels short of a rum run. Thinks he's as tall as his name is long."

For what was likely the first time in years, the corners of Admiral McCray's mouth twisted into the tiniest smile. "And he squints," he added. "As if someone stole his spectacles."

Scarlet gasped, forgetting her reservations at the sight of that smile. "You're right! We did it ourselves, the time we raided the *Dark Ranger* to save Fitz. Pinched 'em right off his snout. Now Tim wears them every day and . . ." Scarlet stopped when she saw her father's look of confusion. Scurvy! She could have kicked herself. "I mean . . . the time we raided their camp. To . . . save Fitz. Yes, he got himself captured, the clumsy oaf. But we saved him, no problem. Barely took a minute."

"You raided their camp?" Admiral McCray's mouth fell back into a frown. "What were you thinking?"

This is precisely why no grown-ups are allowed, Scarlet thought, rolling her eyes.

"Don't roll your eyes at me. This isn't a game. You and your little friends might have been safe on this island until now, but—"

"Father," Scarlet interrupted, "we know how to fend for ourselves."

"But—"

"No buts. I've been taking care of myself for three years."

He opened his mouth to argue again, then shut it. They walked on in silence.

Finally he said, "Apparently the pirates think there's treasure on the island. Rubies or something."

Scarlet tried to look disinterested. "You don't say."

"Treasure. Hmph." Her father frowned harder. "I personally wouldn't care if there were a hundred treasures here. I'd move us out tomorrow if I could."

Before Scarlet could jump in and encourage him to do just that, the creature in distress barged back into her brain. She rubbed her temples. *Deal with your brother yourself, Monkey,* she tried to tell him. *I've got my own family matters to take care of.*

She watched her father trudge along beside her. He was being an old boar, no doubt about it. But when he'd smiled just now, he'd been the old father, if only for a second. Maybe, deep down, he could still remember?

Scarlet drew a breath. "When I came to this island, I couldn't remember it, either. But then I searched inside myself, and everything started coming back to me. I remembered the village and the clearing. And I remembered my mother, too. I'd actually forgotten what she looked like."

The admiral swallowed hard and said nothing, so Scarlet pressed on.

"And you, too, Father. I remembered how I used to sit with you while you carved the Islanders' boats, and you'd make me those little wooden stars. You must remember *that*."

When he finally spoke, his voice sounded strangled. "I don't remember."

Scarlet stopped. "Oh, come *on*—"

"I don't. And what's more, I don't want to."

"Well, I . . ." She couldn't believe it. "You don't have to be such a grump about it! I think it's just awful that you won't even try when—"

"Not another word," he commanded. "I must go see to my men."

"Fine then!" Scarlet cried. "Go!"

"Oh no! Not this time. You're coming with me."

"I most certainly am *not*!"

Scarlet tried to stare him down while mentally composing a list of all the things she'd rather do than go anywhere with him: 1) Eat an entire plate of raw oysters. 2) Memorize the Latin names of every plant on Island X. 3) Clean the long drop for an entire year. 4) . . .

Suddenly he stepped back as if he'd seen something truly frightening. "Fine. Fine then. I have to leave." And he swung around and hurried off the way he'd come.

Scarlet had just turned to look behind her, wondering what could have possibly scared him off, when she was filled with a feeling of panic like none she'd ever felt.

She pressed her hand to her forehead. Either the entire jungle was upset, or this was one powerful creature. "Shivers," she whispered.

That's when she heard the noise. The last noise she would have expected to hear on Island X.

The crack of a gun.

CHAPTER ELEVEN

When Emmett dashed through camp with the news of the approaching King's Man, Jem waited to hear Scarlet's commands come thundering across the clearing. They didn't. On his second lap around the clearing, Emmett added that she'd gone ahead on her own to investigate the intruder.

"What do we do?" Edwin cried.

"Should we hide?" Elmo asked.

The rest of the crew began to fumble for their weapons.

Jem swallowed hard. Once again, the Lost Souls were seriously in need of direction. He quickly assessed the situation and concluded that there wasn't a soul in camp capable of giving it. He swallowed again. It would have to be him.

"Everybody just . . . calm down," he said in his best take-charge voice. A few Lost Souls actually stopped and looked at him. "Um . . ." Jem racked his brain for the next confident-sounding thing to say. "Let's . . . ask the pigs for help?"

The Lost Souls nodded and kept looking at him.

"Oh. You want me to do it?"

"You've talked to them before, haven't you?" said Elmo.

"Well, yes. Good point."

Jem sniffed hard, picked up a scent, and followed it toward the rookery, where he found a wrinkly, hairy, and very smelly wild pig.

It wasn't the chief, to whom Jem had spoken once before, but he decided to give it a go. He hoped all pigs were equally well versed in English. He assumed the same tone that had worked for him the last time.

"Sir. The King's Men are invading our camp, sir. I know that you pigs want nothing to do with them, and frankly we don't, either, but I'm not sure we can fight them off without you . . . sir." Jem looked anxiously at the boar, who grumbled, smacked his lips, then ambled off into the jungle.

Moments later the pig chief emerged. Jem repeated his plea, adding a few more *sirs* and even one *Your Excellency*, hoping that if the pig *had* learned English in the Old World, he'd appreciate this. The chief snorted and sniffed, then let out a tremendous belch.

"Yikes," Jem said. He didn't have Scarlet to translate, but he was fairly certain that meant "No." Now they'd need another plan. He ran back to camp, where everyone was still fumbling with their weapons.

"Where are the pigs?" Sam asked.

Jem shook his head. "I don't think they're coming."

"What do you mean?"

"Are you sure you asked the right way?" asked Edwin. "The way Scarlet does?"

Jem threw up his hands. "I know how to talk to the pigs! I did it in the first place. And I could tell the chief wasn't interested."

"So what now?" asked Sam.

"I say we get ready to ambush." Smitty hoisted his bow up on his shoulder.

Jem didn't want to put his faith in the Deadly Parrot of Death's archery skills, but he didn't have a better plan. "All right," he said reluctantly. "Emmett, which way did you come from?"

Emmett pointed, just as a deafening blast caused everyone to gasp.

"Was that . . . ?" Sam puffed.

"Sounded like a musket." Tim straightened his spectacles and pointed to the right. "Over that way, I think."

Jem's stomach flipped. "The way Scarlet went?"

"And Ronagh and Liam!" cried Emmett. "What do we do?"

"We've got to go make sure they're safe."

The Lost Souls agreed that this was a good idea, but no one moved.

Jem gulped. "All right, follow me, then." And he set off for the edge of the clearing, hoping that they'd follow. What good could he do by himself? A moment later, he heard soft footsteps behind him and turned to see Elmo a few feet behind.

"I'm with ya," Elmo said.

"Thanks." Jem glanced back at the rest of the Lost Souls, who were straightening their trousers and retying their bootlaces, obviously stalling. "So much for strength in numbers." He started off again, Elmo stepping in his boot prints.

They hadn't even reached the edge of the jungle when Ronagh came flying out of it, one hand covering her mouth.

"Ronagh! What is it?" Jem reached out to grab her sleeve.

But the little girl wrenched her arm away and kept running. The boys exchanged a nervous glance and continued on.

They found Liam crouching behind a tree not far from the clearing. He motioned them to get down. "Where's Ronagh?"

Jem pointed back toward the camp. "What happened? Where's the King's Man?"

At that point, Scarlet arrived, puffing and panting. She dropped to her knees beside them.

"What's going on?" she gasped.

"It's the King's Men," Liam whispered. "Ronagh and I spotted two after you left."

"Blast," Scarlet whispered. "They must have followed him."

"Followed who?" asked Elmo.

Scarlet shook her head. "Then what happened?"

"We spied on them for a bit," Liam continued. "Then we saw a smelly wild pig cross their path."

"And chase them off?" Scarlet asked hopefully.

Liam shook his head and swallowed hard. "One of the King's Men had a musket." He put his finger to his lips, peeked around the tree, and pointed. Perhaps thirty yards away, three King's Men were crouched over something enormous and gray and deathly still. They seemed to be discussing how to move it back to their camp.

"Scurvy, blast, and blimey." Scarlet sank back behind the tree and smacked her forehead.

"What do we do now?" Elmo asked.

Scarlet looked at them each in turn, then replied, "We get those murderers away from our camp. What have we got to fight them off with?"

The boys looked at one another dubiously. Elmo produced a small dagger. Liam pulled out his slingshot.

Without a word, Scarlet grabbed Liam's weapon and slipped away before anyone could point out that a slingshot couldn't very well take on a musket. Jem's stomach pitched like it had on the high seas, back in the days when he and Uncle Finn . . .

"Uncle Finn," Jem whispered. Why hadn't he thought of him before? He should have called Uncle Finn and Thomas ages ago.

"Is he close by?" asked Elmo.

"I don't know," Jem replied, suddenly realizing that he hadn't seen Uncle Finn or Thomas since the previous morning when he'd left them cataloging plants. He couldn't believe they'd have gone off exploring without telling him. So where *were* they? An ominous feeling crept into his churning stomach. It was too late and far too dangerous to go look for them. Jem reached into his pocket and touched the pipe, but he knew that its noise would only draw attention. And possibly shatter a few eardrums.

They watched Scarlet dart from tree to tree until she was about ten yards away from the King's Men, at which point she picked up a stone and nestled it into the clamshell. Then she pulled back and shot it at the head of the man bent over the dead pig.

The stone whizzed right by the man's ear, and he yelped, looking around wildly. But Scarlet dove into a leafy shrub, out of sight.

The King's Man yelled to his comrades, who looked up from the pig to scan the jungle. Jem saw Scarlet's skinny arm reach out and nab another stone from the forest floor.

Be careful, Scarlet, he told her silently. *Be*—

Then suddenly an arrow came zinging from somewhere behind him. It practically sang as it zipped through the air, straight toward the King's Men. Before any of them knew what was happening, the man farthest to the right found his coat sleeve pinned to the tree behind him. His jaw dropped, and his companions howled in terror.

"Smitty?" Jem turned. The boy must have followed him and Elmo after all. And somehow become an amazing shot in just a day.

But Smitty was nowhere to be seen. In fact, all that could be seen—and heard and smelled—were a few dozen smelly wild pigs galloping toward him, tusks skimming the dirt. Their hoofbeats drowned out the King's Men's bellows for help. Their smell spread through the jungle like fire through a dry forest. Liam and Elmo ducked and covered their heads so the pigs wouldn't trample them, but Jem kept his up, wanting to watch.

Two of the King's Men dropped everything and

hightailed it back the way they'd come. The third, however, remained pinned to the tree, squirming and screaming at the approaching pigs. Just an instant before the chief skewered his knees, the man slipped out of his coat and dashed off after his comrades, leaving the coat behind.

Several pigs galloped after them. But a few others, the chief included, halted right where the King's Men had stood.

Jem bit his lip. He wondered how long it had been since a pig had been killed on Island X.

The chief looked from the retreating King's Men to Scarlet shuffling toward him. Then he looked down at the body before him and let out a long, throaty moan.

There was no need for anyone to translate. Everyone could tell what the chief was thinking.

"I've never been to a funeral for a person before," Smitty confided to Jem. "Much less one for an animal." Only an hour had passed since the pig had been killed, and already the two stood waist-deep in the grave they were digging for it.

Jem stopped to wipe away the sweat trickling into his eyes. "Much less one for a pig."

"Sure is a shame," said Smitty.

"Hey, Smit, when was the last time you saw Uncle Finn and Thomas?" Jem leaned on his shovel, which Tim had brought up from the *Hop* on one of his visits.

"Hmm." Smitty stopped digging. "I'd say yesterday

morning. Maybe a few hours before the spying mission. Why? Did they go looking for bromly-things?"

"I don't know." Jem sighed and started digging again. "I guess they must have. But you'd think they would have told me."

Smitty clicked his tongue against his teeth. "I'll bet they're just off exploring. They'll be back any minute now. Maybe Thomas'll have grown feathers this time!"

"Yeah. Probably." Jem forced a smile, although he wasn't convinced. "Nice shot today, by the way."

"What's that?"

"Your arrow. The one that pinned the King's Man to the tree."

"My arrow?" Smitty repeated, looking confused. "Really? I thought I missed."

"Missed?"

"Uh-huh. I took a shot, but I was pretty far away, and I thought it flew straight into the dirt. But you say it pinned the King's Man to a tree?"

"Well, yes," Jem said, puzzled. "Didn't you see?" Smitty shook his head. "It was a perfect shot."

"Huh." Smitty considered this, then grinned. "Guess I'm more talented than I give myself credit for. Jolly!"

"I guess . . ." The story didn't quite add up, but they had no time to discuss it further. The funeral was about to begin.

The funeral had been Ronagh's idea. Or rather, Ronagh's command. After her tears had dried and her sniffles subsided, she took on the role of funeral director. No one dared argue. Scarlet insisted they bury the body, since burning it would attract attention. So they chose a spot downwind of the clearing.

Scarlet now stood off to the side, watching the funeral preparations and looking as dejected as Jem had ever seen her. Once the grave was dug, he went to stand beside her.

At first she said nothing. Then, finally, she tore her eyes away from the Lost Souls rolling the corpse into the pit. "They're furious, Fitz."

"The pigs?" He looked over at the band, which had gathered for the ceremony.

She nodded.

"At us?" Jem swallowed hard.

Scarlet sighed. "At everyone and everything. They won't help us again. They don't even want us to ask."

Jem thought about this for a moment. "Well, I don't blame them. But this pig wasn't killed in battle. He was killed because—"

"Because those biscuit-eating King's Men think they own the whole world and can do whatever they please!" A voice piped up behind them. They turned to see Monty stamping his foot on the grass.

"They're worse than biscuit-eaters!" Edwin spat. "They're bacon-eaters."

A few Lost Souls nodded and murmured in agreement.

"They're Enemy Number One," Gil proclaimed.

More murmurs.

Jem turned back to Scarlet, whose face had turned an odd shade of olive. But before he could ask if she was going to be sick, Ronagh bellowed for everyone's attention and began the funeral ceremony. A cloud drifted over to obscure the sun, darkening the afternoon even more.

The ceremony was short and simple and involved a few Lost Souls stepping forward to say some nice words about the deceased. The problem was, none of them had known him at all. And the pigs didn't seem up to sharing their own thoughts.

"He was brave and fierce," offered Charlie.

"With very pointy horns," Elmo said.

"Tusks," Jem corrected him.

"Tusks." Elmo clasped his hands and bowed his head solemnly.

"And he didn't really smell all that bad . . . once you got used to it," Smitty added.

Then they sang one of the only songs they all knew well, "The Ballad of Salty Jack," and then filled in the grave with dirt and leaves. Once the victim had been laid to rest, the pigs began to wander off, leaving the Lost Souls to wonder what the flotsam they were going to do next.

CHAPTER TWELVE

That night, the clouds that had gathered throughout the afternoon began to rumble and roll. A few hours before daylight, a crack of thunder split them open, and great, big raindrops began to fall, soaking everything and everyone in the clearing. Sodden and sullen, the Lost Souls picked up their cloaks and headed for the trees, where they huddled, shivering, until the rain subsided at dawn.

Soaked to the bone, Jem gnawed anxiously on some guava fruit. Two great, big worries were bouncing around his brain: 1) the tree houses he ought to have built by now and 2) Uncle Finn and Thomas—wet, lost, or at the mercy of some treasure-hungry pirates.

"All right." He swallowed the last of his breakfast and shook some raindrops from his hair. "Sitting here worrying isn't going to help. I should either start building the houses or go look for Uncle Finn."

Reasoning that he'd do a terrible job of the houses with Uncle Finn's disappearance on his mind, Jem chose the second option.

He looked around at the Lost Souls, who were creeping back into the clearing now that the rain had stopped. Thankfully, Scarlet was in camp and not off chasing some monkey or iguana, so the crew was finally getting some direction. One group was getting ready for a second spying mission while another gathered to learn the fine art of archery from Smitty. He wouldn't be missed for some time.

Although he didn't like to rely on the island to steer him, Jem hadn't a clue which direction to take. So he chose randomly and set off, scanning the jungle for clues of the explorers' whereabouts. He'd only wandered a little way, however, when a nearby bush rustled. Jem startled, cursing himself for setting out alone. Then he looked at the culprit. It was none other than Gil Jenkins.

Gil's eyes widened at the sight of him. "Fitz!"

"Gil! What are you doing here?"

It would have been a perfectly logical question to ask almost anyone he met in the depths of the jungle. But not Gil. The boy's surprise quickly turned to anger.

"Seriously, Fitz? You always have to ask? To do my business, all right?"

"All right, all right, don't get your trousers in a knot." Jem stepped aside to let him pass. "Sheesh." He heard Gil retreating deeper into the jungle. Eventually his footsteps faded away.

Jem continued on, calling Uncle Finn's name. But he'd gone only a few dozen steps farther when something else made him stop. Something small and silver lying on the ground before him. Something he hadn't for the life of him expected to see again.

"My knife!" He turned. "Hey! Gil!" But Gil was long gone.

Jem turned back to the knife. "What on earth . . . hey!" he shouted again as he spotted a monkey inching toward it. The creature's hair stood up on one side of its head—rather like Jem's own some mornings. It reached for the knife.

"Oh no you don't!" Jem dove for it, but the monkey was faster. It snatched up the knife and bounded off, shrieking.

"Come back here!" Jem stumbled after it. "I *won't* lose my knife again!"

He ran hard, dodging trees and hurdling ferns, managing to stay on the monkey's tail until it suddenly leaped off the ground. The monkey hurtled through the air with a triumphant screech and landed on the shoulder of a young boy.

Jem came to a grinding halt. No more than seven years old, the boy had dark eyes and an eager grin. He wore no shirt—just a ragged pair of Old World trousers cut at the knee and cinched with a rope at his waist. Never in his life had Jem seen the boy before.

"Who?" he gasped. Then a thought hit him like a football in the face. He gasped again. "You're not an Islander, are you?"

The boy just smiled and shushed the monkey jabbering in his ear. Then he plucked the knife from the monkey's fingers and held it out to Jem. The monkey proceeded to throw a temper tantrum on his shoulder.

Jem reached out and accepted his knife, and his fingers brushed the boy's. "But . . . I thought you . . . you all died after . . . ," Jem sputtered.

Suddenly something came crashing through the

bushes, and both Jem and the boy turned to see a girl with bare arms and long black hair, perhaps a year or two older than Jem. She had the same dark eyes as the boy and wore a dress made of palm leaves woven together with pieces of cloth that might once have been an Old World coat—a familiar-looking one, at that. Tiny, delicate vines twisted around her wrists and ankles, and she had a bow slung over her shoulder. When she saw Jem, she froze.

"Shivers," Jem breathed.

The little boy looked from him to the girl with a nervous smile. The monkey leaped off into the bushes.

For a moment Jem and the girl could only stare at each other. Then, finally, she turned to the boy and said a few words. Although she spoke in a language Jem had never heard before, her tone made him certain she was saying something along the lines of, "What the flotsam do you think you're doing?" Then she snatched the boy up under one arm and zipped back into the bushes.

"Wait!" Jem called. "Come back! I won't hurt you!" But they disappeared without a sound to indicate where they'd gone.

"You've *got* to be joking." All thoughts of tree houses, pirates, and King's Men fled Jem's brain as quickly as the pair had disappeared. They *must* have been Islanders— real, live Islanders. And they *were* real—Jem had reached out and touched one.

"This. Is. Amazing," he said. He wondered what it would take for Scarlet to believe him.

"I don't believe you."

"I didn't think you would."

"You're joking."

"I'm not." Jem crossed his heart. "I wouldn't have believed it myself if I hadn't seen them. Right up close."

"Seen what?" Smitty paused in passing. "Cap'n, you look as if you've seen a ghost."

"A ghost!" Scarlet snapped her fingers. "That's it. They must have been spirits."

Jem shook his head. "I touched one. They were real."

"What were real?" Smitty looked back and forth between them.

Scarlet ignored him. "But the Islanders are dead. Everyone knows that."

Jem shrugged. "These two weren't. Look, Captain, I know they're Islanders. I'd bet the *Hop* on it. In fact, I'd bet *Uncle Finn* on it."

"Islanders?" Smitty shouted. "There are Islanders on Island X?"

Several other Lost Souls in the clearing looked up.

"Islanders? Where?"

Within seconds, Scarlet and Jem were surrounded, being bombarded with questions.

"Captain, what's going on?" Liam asked.

Jem answered for her, quickly summing up his story to the other Lost Souls as they stared at him, mouths open like flying fish.

"Are you sure?" Tim asked. "Because . . . well . . . the Islanders are dead, mate."

Jem took a deep breath. "I know. I know that's what we've been told. But you only need to look at Scarlet to know that not all the Islanders died of the fever."

The Lost Souls' heads swiveled to Scarlet, who was looking seriously perplexed.

"So you're saying they've been here? All along?" Edwin's voice dripped with doubt.

"Exactly. And it explains so much," Jem said. "Like why things keep disappearing!"

"You think they're stealing from us?" Scarlet, too, sounded dubious.

"Well, I—"

"What's all this?"

All heads now turned to Gil, who'd just appeared on the scene, looking flushed and out of breath. Someone near the back of the crowd brought him up to speed.

Gil's eyebrows disappeared under his flop of brown hair. "Islanders? But that's impossible. They're all dead."

"These two," Jem said, tired of repeating himself, "were not at all dead."

"Really? You're sure you'd know an Islander if you saw one? No offense, Jem, but you're pretty Old World."

Old World! Jem had had enough. He took a step toward Gil. "I'm no more Old World than any of you," he declared, then added, "with the obvious exception." He nodded at Scarlet. "I saw two Islanders today. I'm not lying."

But Gil didn't back down. He, too, raised his voice. "Don't you get mad at me, Fitzgerald. I'm not in the mood!" He stepped closer to Jem until they were standing nearly nose to nose.

Jem dragged his eyes away from Gil and looked at the crowd of dirty faces. Not a single Lost Soul seemed to believe him. "This is ridiculous," he said, and he turned and walked away.

"Stupid, stupid pirates," he muttered, stomping hard on the grass, not caring how sacred it was. "'You're too Old World to know an Islander, Jem.' *Humph*. Like they'd know an Islander and I wouldn't."

He could still picture them perfectly. The girl wore a dress made out of plants and an Old World coat . . . Jem snapped his fingers. The coat that had disappeared from Scarlet's pile of belongings. And she'd blamed the monkey!

"We must have been chasing one of them the other day!"

And on her shoulder she'd had—

"That's it!" Jem snapped his fingers again, picturing the girl's bow. *She* was the one who had shot at the King's Man and pinned his coat to the tree. He knew it couldn't have been Smitty!

Feeling like a brilliant detective, Jem turned around and marched back to the clearing. He would show the crew what had been under their noses all along.

CHAPTER THIRTEEN

It wasn't that Scarlet didn't want to believe Jem. Her brain was just so full of questions (When to pay attention to a creature in distress? How to teach the aras to hang on to their rubies? How to fight off and/or attack Lucas and his crew? What the flotsam to do about her father?) that she feared one more might make it explode.

But the look on Jem's face when he returned to the clearing told her she had better take this one seriously. If he was right and there really were Islanders on Island X, it would change everything.

"All right, Fitz," she said. "Show me."

She told the spying mission to wait a few minutes and followed Jem into the jungle—to the spot where the King's Man had killed the pig the day before.

"Look. There are two arrows here. There's this one." He picked up an arrow from the jungle floor. Too thick and crooked to fly in a straight line, it had obviously been carved clumsily and in haste. "And there's that one over there." He led her to the tree where the King's Man's coat still hung. "This second one is perfect. You can't tell me it belongs to Smitty. I know he means well, but he's no fletcher." When Scarlet raised an eyebrow, he added, "That's an Old World name for someone who makes arrows."

Scarlet's stomach turned a somersault. The second

arrow was straight and smooth, its head a sharp black stone.

"Captain," Jem said seriously, "this was the job of an expert."

Scarlet bit her lip and whispered, "You're right." She looked from the arrow to Jem. "But then . . . where are they?"

"I don't know," Jem said. "But I'm starting to think they're never far away."

Scarlet shook her head in amazement. Islanders, here all along, and she hadn't even felt their presence. "They must be first-class spies," she murmured. And she couldn't help but wonder if they'd recognized her.

Jem nodded. "I bet the girl will be back for her arrow and this coat, too. She seems to make her clothes out of Old World cloth and plants. Actually, I think she used your coat for her dress."

"My coat!" Scarlet cried. "My stolen coat?"

Jem nodded. "So maybe we should wait here until they come back, although who knows how long that'll be."

"A girl and her brother," Scarlet said. Who were they? Could they be childhood friends? Or . . . cousins? Dazed, she nodded. If there really were Islanders on Island X, she had to meet them—even if it meant putting the pirates on hold for an hour or two.

She chose a large plant with heart-shaped leaves and crouched behind it, moving over so Jem could sit beside her.

"I hope this works," he whispered.

They rustled around, checking for snakes and spiders and getting comfortable on the forest floor. Then they settled into silence, passing the time by watching leaf-cutter ants march single file across the dirt. Each one carried a tiny piece of a leaf on its back. Scarlet felt their stoic determination, and it reminded her of the King's Men.

That brought her father to mind. His refusal to remember his past still made her want to throw things. If he would only try, it would all come back to him—of that she was certain. Maddening, maddening grown-up.

Grown-ups. Scarlet sat up straight as a wild and wonderful thought came to mind. If these children were indeed Islanders, could some grown-ups have survived as well? Namely, her mother?

Don't get your hopes up, she told herself firmly. One thing at a time. And yet, wouldn't it be amazing . . .

Jem's head lolled beside her, and she poked him in the ribs to wake him up. He grimaced and crossed his eyes. Scarlet stifled a laugh and touched her tongue to her nose. Jem puffed out his cheeks and pulled on his ears. Scarlet flipped her eyelids inside out.

Jem looked horrified. "That's disgusting!"

"Shhh!" Scarlet raised her finger to her lips, then noticed the nice shadow it made on a nearby tree. Jem noticed it, too. He twisted his hands into the shape of a bird in flight and made the shadow fly across the tree trunk.

"Jolly!" Scarlet mouthed. She added a bouncing rabbit to the scene. Then Jem transformed his bird into a dog and turned it on her rabbit. A frenzied chase ensued, and they were mere seconds away from bursting into laughter when they heard a soft padding just beyond the ferns. Rabbit and dog froze in mid-chase, and they slowly, soundlessly, turned back into fingers. Scarlet parted the ferns as quietly as she could and looked out.

Her stomach turned another somersault at the sight: A girl, perhaps a year older than her, was sneaking toward the arrow in the tree. She had long black hair like Scarlet's, but without the tangles. Behind her trotted a boy, even smaller than the smallest Lost Soul. Scarlet's heart began to pound again. Jem nudged her, mouthing, "Do something."

Trembling, she rose and cleared her throat. "Hello."

The children whirled around to face her. Jem stood up as well. The girl, caught with her hand on the arrow, froze for a moment, then in one swift motion yanked it from the tree, grabbed her bow, and drew its string back to her eye, pointing the arrow right at Scarlet's face.

"Oh!" Scarlet threw her hands up. "Don't do that! We don't mean any harm. We . . . oh scurvy." *Now would be a perfect time to remember my old language*, she thought, taking a slow step back from the pointy object aimed at her nose.

Beside her, Jem raised his arms as well. "Can you talk to them?" he hissed.

"Obviously not, or I'd be doing it!" Scarlet shot back. *Think, think, think*, she urged herself. But no words came.

The girl muttered something to her brother, then motioned for him to get behind her. They began to move backward.

"Wait! Don't go!" Scarlet stepped forward and found herself with an arrow an inch away from her left eye. "Okaaaay . . ." She stepped back again. Blasted memory. Blasted language. Blasted father for making her forget. She decided to try English, anyway. "Look, I'm Scarlet . . . I mean, Ara! My Islander name is Ara. And this is Fitz, er . . . Jem. We don't want to harm you, I swear. We're here to protect the island. You see, it's my home, too. You might not remember, but we probably all grew up together."

The girl blinked but didn't lower her weapon.

"I don't think she remembers," Jem whispered.

"Thanks, Fitz," Scarlet replied through clenched teeth. She decided to simplify things. Poking herself in the chest, she said, "Ara." Poking Jem, she said, "Jem."

The girl muttered something to her brother, who nodded and replied.

"What do you think they're saying?" Jem whispered.

The girl gave Scarlet a scornful look, gestured to her trousers and dirty shirt, then shook her head at the boy. Scarlet's ears burned. Whatever it was, it certainly wasn't the warm welcome she would have liked.

But before she could say anything more, the children turned and zipped off into the jungle.

"Wait!" Scarlet gasped. "Don't go!"

"Should we go after them?" Jem looked ready for another chase.

Scarlet shook her head. "If we chase them, it'll just scare them even more."

"Oh." He looked dejected. "But if we don't, no one'll believe us."

Scarlet watched some branches shake where the Islanders had pushed through them. She remembered the way the children had looked at her and how it felt to flounder for words she had completely forgotten.

Her anger began to simmer again.

"I'm going for a walk," she announced. And she turned to her right and pushed her way into the trees.

"Oh. Okay," Jem said to her back.

He began to say something else, but she ignored it. She only had one thing on her mind: The sole person on Island X who could help her remember what he had once made her forget. If he would only try.

It was early afternoon by the time Scarlet reached the cluster of gray canvas tents. She stopped and looked around, suddenly realizing that marching up to her father and demanding some language lessons might not be as simple as it sounded. First off, she had to find him without attracting his crew's attention. A few King's Men were chatting off to her right, so she sneaked toward them for clues.

"Come on, Donovan," a young man sitting on an overturned pail said to another standing before him. Scarlet recognized the one seated as the yellow-bellied boy she'd followed through the jungle a few days before.

"You're sure you didn't imagine the whole thing?"

"Imagine it? *Imagine it?*" the other man exclaimed. "You think I just left my coat behind by accident? Ask Collins and Watt. They saw it." He stepped toward the man on the pail. "Listen to me. Us and those pirates, we aren't the only ones on this island."

"So there are spirits," the yellow-belly scoffed. "How much harm can they do? I say we march right back there and drag that pig home. I'm hungry."

Donovan shook his head. "Not me. No, sir. You can face those spirits—or whatever they are—yourself."

The yellow-belly laughed. "What did the admiral say when you told him?" He jerked his thumb toward a very large tent off to Scarlet's left.

That was just too easy, she thought, and turned in that direction.

Donovan harrumphed. "Told me that next time we follow him without his permission, he'll see to it that we never leave camp again."

Good, Scarlet thought. *Although I personally would keelhaul you.*

The yellow-belly snorted. "At least he'll be gone soon. If you ask me, the old man should've retired years ago." Donovan shushed him.

Retired? Scarlet paused. The admiral? Had the life of a King's Man finally worn him out? She shook her head; she had more pressing things to think about.

Once hidden in the bushes beside his tent, she thought hard and fast. What would get his attention and draw him out? The idea that came to mind wasn't exactly creative, but it would do. She began to search the ground for pebbles and lobbed them at her father's tent.

Sure enough, moments later, out he stomped, scowling left and right.

Scarlet poked her head out of the bushes. "Father."

His eyes fell upon her, and his mouth fell open.

"Scarlet!" he hissed, moving toward her. "What are you doing here?"

"Meet me in the clearing," she whispered, slithering backward out of the bushes.

He met her there within minutes, breathing hard. "Scarlet, this is dangerous. You shouldn't be—"

"I know, I know."

"No, you don't know. One of my men was almost killed yesterday. Nearly had his arm taken off by . . ." His voice trailed off as he watched her reaction. "Scarlet, tell me you weren't involved with that."

"Well, I can tell you I didn't shoot at him. But he deserved it after what he did. Killing the smelly wild pig and all."

"Smelly wild pig!" the admiral exclaimed, then lowered his voice again. "This isn't a game, Scarlet. This is serious."

Scarlet took a deep breath to calm her temper. "Father. I need your help. This is more important than your man getting pegged to a tree."

He raised his eyebrows. "What is it?"

She paused, then blurted out, "I need you to teach me the Islander language again."

"You need . . . what?" He looked bewildered. "Why?

Scarlet, I don't remember any of that. It's gone." He said the last two words as if each one weighed a ton, then looked away.

"Look, this is important. Couldn't you at least try?" She considered telling him about the Islander children but decided against it. What if he wanted to see them? That would just frighten them even more.

"Try? No, I can't try. It's a waste of time!"

"Please? I know that if you thought hard—"

He shook his head. "No. There's nothing left in me. I don't remember."

"It *is* in you," Scarlet insisted, not caring that she was raising her voice. "I found memories inside me even though you tried to erase them all. Blimey, Father, I had even forgotten my own mother!"

The admiral spun to face her. "Don't you bring her into this! I won't talk about her."

"Well, I—"

"You don't understand." His voice was hard and jagged like his face. "You can't begin to understand what it's like knowing that you were the reason your wife and her entire family, her entire *village* died."

Scarlet froze. "What? What are you talking about?"

He turned away again, and his shoulders sagged.

"*You* didn't do it, Father," Scarlet whispered, her anger fading fast. "You didn't bring the fever yourself."

He rubbed his forehead. "It doesn't matter whether it was me or the next King's Man or all of us. I was part of the problem. And I have to live with that every day."

Scarlet wanted to reach for his hand, but he looked so full of anguish, so old, that it seemed like a single touch might shatter him. So she could only stand there until finally he straightened and turned back to her.

"I can't remember," he said. "And I can't be here any more. I have to get off the island."

"You mean you're moving your men?"

"I mean I'm leaving the tropics."

Scarlet started. "I'm sorry?"

"I'm retiring. I told my men this morning. I'm going back to the Old World."

Scarlet could only stare. She'd now officially received too much information for one day.

"And I expect you to meet me here tomorrow. Spend one more night with your friends if you must."

"My . . ."

"You'll meet me here tomorrow. We'll leave promptly."

Leave? For the Old World? Scarlet's jaw dropped. "But . . . I can't come with you."

"Now *that* is not up to you," he said curtly. "As my daughter, you'll do as you're told."

Scarlet felt dizzy. "I can't," she said again. "This is my home. My crew is here and—"

"Your crew? Scarlet, be serious. You may have spent the last few years playing with some street children, but that's not how you're going to live from now on."

"Playing with street children!" Scarlet cried. "How dare you! My mates are the bravest, most tireless—" she stopped, partly because she was about to give away their identity and partly because she was fairly certain her brain was about to explode.

"I leave tomorrow," said the admiral. "I trust you'll be here to meet me."

Then he turned and walked back to his camp, leaving Scarlet utterly speechless.

CHAPTER FOURTEEN

Scarlet staggered away from the clearing, feeling as if she'd just been run over by a schooner. She wasn't sure what was more disturbing: her father assuming she'd pack up and return to the Old World or her father blaming himself for the Islanders' deaths.

All these years he'd been carrying that awful guilt. Scarlet couldn't begin to imagine what that felt like. No wonder he didn't want to rustle up old memories.

And yet, she wondered, did that excuse him for trying to forget? And forcing her to forget, too? She wasn't sure.

After a while she stopped and looked around to determine just where she was. This business of relying on the island to direct her was just plain tiresome. She really had to get back to the Lost Souls. She'd been gone the better part of the day, and they'd be getting antsy by now.

"Speaking of antsy," she said as her eyes fell on a familiar line of leaf-cutter ants. "Maybe if I followed—"

"Captain!" Jem's voice floated through the trees.

"Fitz!" Scarlet cried, looking up. "Where are you?"

"Right here." He popped out from behind a nearby tree, wearing a grin she wouldn't have expected on someone who'd made the discovery of a lifetime but couldn't convince his mates it had happened.

"Tell me you have good news. I *need* good news."

Jem shook his head. "I don't have good news, Scarlet.

I have *great* news. I think I've finally got it."

"Got what?" The sight of a happy crew member filled Scarlet with such hope that she was able to crack a joke. "No, let me guess. The cure for baldness."

"Better."

"Feather beds for everyone!"

"Uh-uh. I know where the Islanders live."

Scarlet gasped. "What? Where? How did you figure it out?"

"Well, I went back to the clearing and consulted my map. And I noticed something I drew yesterday morning. A clue!"

"What?" Scarlet was dying to know.

"Liam's squash helmet."

"Liam's squash . . ." She shook her head, mystified.

"The Islanders must grow them!" Jem jabbed a finger in the air.

Scarlet gasped. "You think so?"

Jem nodded, whipping out his map and unfurling it with a flourish. "Now all we have to do is find the squash. And by my calculations, it's this way." He turned and marched off. Scarlet followed, reflecting that maybe a map wasn't such a bad thing to have around.

A few minutes later, they came upon the root she'd tripped over twice. (Thankfully, this time she avoided it.)

"Here's the root. So the squash should be right . . . there." Jem pointed to some short plants with jagged leaves. The tree canopy was thinner there, so the sun could speckle them with its late-afternoon light.

Scarlet stared at the plants, and after a moment she

realized that they were growing in distinct rows.

"It's a garden!" She kneeled to part the leaves, revealing two bright-orange gourds. Suddenly, memories of roasted vegetables flashed through her brain. Of course the Islanders gardened! "You're brilliant, Fitz."

"Thanks." He blushed. "So I guess their house can't be far away . . ."

They spun slowly, surveying the jungle around them.

Scarlet gasped. "Would you look at that?"

Jem gaped. "Sink me! Now *there's* a tree house."

A small, sturdy hut perched in the branches of an enormous tree some fifteen yards off the ground. Its roof was covered in big, flat leaves that helped it blend into its surroundings.

"*That* is exactly what we need," said Jem. "I wonder if they're home."

He didn't have to wonder long. A face soon appeared in the doorway, then the little boy popped out. After looking around cautiously, he grinned at Scarlet and Jem and unrolled a swinging ladder made of vines. He scrambled down the ladder to the jungle floor and trotted over to see them.

"Well, that's one warm welcome," Scarlet said. "Now I wonder where . . ."

"Kapu!" A shrill voice reverberated through the trees, and suddenly the boy's sister was sprinting their way, looking as if she might slay them on the spot. Scarlet and Jem threw their arms in the air. The boy slowed to a stop and looked nervously between them and his sister.

"Oh!" Scarlet cried, for suddenly her brain was

flooded with the strongest, clearest feeling of distress—one she'd felt only once before. "Shivers," she whispered as she looked at the girl. "That was *you* I felt when the pig was killed! But how . . . ?"

The girl's fists were clenched so tightly that her knuckles had turned white. Scarlet could practically hear her heart thudding.

I can't believe it, she thought. *I can channel the Islanders even more clearly than the animals. Then maybe this means . . .*

Squeezing her eyes shut, she tried her best to reach the children through her thoughts. *We're not here to hurt you*, she told them silently. *Please. We're here to help.*

The boy and girl looked startled. They looked at each other, then at Scarlet. Then the boy said something to his sister, whose fists slowly unclenched.

"What just happened?" Jem whispered. Scarlet didn't answer; she was holding her breath.

The boy said something else, and the girl shook her head. They spoke some more, then fell silent, staring hard at each other. It was as fierce a staring contest as Scarlet had ever seen—even worse than the ones she used to have with Lucas. After a minute or two, the girl broke first, looking away from her brother and Scarlet and Jem.

The boy turned to Scarlet and Jem with a satisfied smile, poked himself in the chest, and said, "Kapu." Then he poked his sister in the ribs and said, "Sina."

"Ow!" the girl cried. She nailed her brother in the arm.

"Sina and Kapu." Scarlet said their names out loud,

hoping that they'd trigger a memory. But nothing came to mind.

"This tree house"—Jem pointed—"is amazing!"

Kapu nodded, grabbed Jem's sleeve, and led him toward it. Sina stepped forward as if to protest, then sighed and let the boys go. She folded her arms across her chest and glowered.

Upon reaching the big tree, Kapu scaled the swinging ladder and motioned for Jem to follow.

Jem hooted. "Can you believe this?" he called back to Scarlet, then he grabbed the ladder and climbed up after Kapu.

Scarlet felt relieved. He was a good sort, this Kapu. She wanted to go, too, but Sina wasn't moving, so she stayed put.

A warm breeze wove through the trees, bringing with it a waft of spice. Scarlet sniffed deeply. "That's jolly," she said for the sake of conversation, even if Sina couldn't understand.

Sina only grunted.

"Right." Scarlet looked around for something else to talk about, and her eyes settled on some sticks leaning against a tree trunk. Each one was forked about halfway up, and Scarlet studied them for a moment before it suddenly came to her. "Stilts!"

Sina looked at her sharply.

"Stilts!" Scarlet repeated, gesturing toward them. "You walk on them, right?" She attempted to mime what that would look like. Sina only stared until Scarlet began to feel rather ridiculous and stopped miming.

Suddenly, Sina grasped Scarlet's wrist and yanked her toward the stilts. She grabbed a six-foot-long pair for herself and thrust a similar pair at Scarlet. Steadying herself against a tree, she settled her feet into the footholds halfway up the stick.

Thinking that this would be a rather inconvenient time to break her neck, Scarlet followed suit. She secured her feet, said a quick prayer to whichever Islander spirits were watching, then let go of the tree.

She wobbled, but didn't fall. "Okay," she gasped, and took a shaky step forward. The next step felt steadier, and with the third she was practically a stilt master. "Hey!" she shouted to Sina, who stood a few yards away. "Hey, I can do this!"

For the first time, Sina smiled. Then she produced a ball made of leaves wrapped in twine. And without a word of warning, she lobbed it straight at Scarlet.

"Ack!" Scarlet caught it, wobbled dangerously, then straightened. "Ha-ha!" She tossed the ball back. Still grinning, Sina threw it again—harder this time.

"Oh yeah?" Scarlet hurled it back. "You think you can beat me at—"

And that's when it came to her.

"*Tapo,*" she said. The Islander word for their game.

Sina dropped the ball and froze. After a long moment, she began to nod—slowly, then faster. Then she took two giant steps toward Scarlet, reached out, and grabbed her hand. "*Tapo!*"

Scarlet searched every corner of her brain but couldn't find any more words. She closed her eyes and tried her best to tell Sina that she couldn't remember anything more.

After a long moment, a response slipped into her brain and announced itself with amazing clarity.

I'll teach you.

Scarlet opened her eyes. Smiling, the older girl pointed to a nearby tree and told Scarlet its name. Then she did the same with the garden and the tree house. Soon they were running around on their stilts, Sina pointing and shouting out words, and Scarlet shouting them back, slowly beginning to relearn her first language. Within minutes they had a language all their own—a curious, wonderful mixture of words and shared thoughts.

They were so absorbed in it that they almost trampled Kapu and Jem, who'd descended from the tree house.

Sina called something down to Kapu, and his eyes lit up. Scarlet could tell his response meant something along the lines of "I knew it all along."

Jem squinted up at Scarlet. "I didn't know you could walk on stilts."

"Me neither, Fitz!" She laughed as she and Sina both climbed down. "I never would have guessed."

"Huh." He looked puzzled. "Well, anyway, you really should see this tree house, Captain. The design is flawless. Do you think they'd come back to camp and show us how it's done?"

"Good question." Scarlet smiled, eager to show off her new skill. "I'll ask." Through a mixture of words and thoughts, Scarlet asked the Islanders to accompany them back to camp.

Jem jumped at the sound of the Islander words leaving Scarlet's mouth. Then he shook his head. "I think I could be friends with you for a lifetime and never get used to your surprises."

The Islanders were deep in conversation. Kapu seemed eager to go, Sina less so.

"Please?" Scarlet asked her. "You'll really like the crew. And we sure could use your help."

Sina hesitated. "But they're so . . . Old World."

"But they're also children, and they're jolly," Scarlet assured her. "They won't hurt you. If anything, they'll adore you." She hoped Smitty wouldn't be wearing one of his island warrior getups when they arrived.

Sina still looked uncertain, but she gave in when Kapu began to lead the way, bringing with him two sets of stilts to help build the tree houses.

They recounted their stories on the way back to camp, and Scarlet did her best to translate for Jem, who still looked a bit stunned by her latest talent. It turned out that Sina, Kapu, and a few of the elders had been immune to the Island Fever, surviving while all the others perished. The elders had passed on over the years, though, leaving the pair to fend for themselves.

"So no other grown-ups survived?" Scarlet had to ask.

Sina shook her head. "None."

"None," Scarlet repeated slowly, swallowing her disappointment. She knew it had been unlikely, but hearing it for certain was harder than she'd thought it would be. To distract herself, she began to tell the

Islanders about the Lost Souls' mission as pirates and their new mission as guardians of Island X and the treasure everyone was after.

"Treasure?" Kapu asked. "What treasure?"

"Those rubies in the aras' nests," Scarlet replied.

The Islanders burst out laughing. "Those old rocks?"

Scarlet explained that Old Worlders thought rubies were precious and even traded them for other valuable things like ships and weapons.

Sina and Kapu shook their heads in disbelief.

"So all those men we've been spying on came for the red rocks?" Kapu asked.

"Sort of. The pirates—the scruffier ones—know about the rubies. They just don't know where to find them. The King's Men—the ones in blue coats—came for things like wood, spices, and maybe even aras. But we're afraid they'll find out about the rubies, too."

"Sina pegged one of the blue coats to the tree yesterday after the man killed the pig!" Kapu said proudly.

Scarlet nodded. "That's what we figured. Well, actually Jem figured it out himself. Excellent shot, by the way."

Sina shrugged as if trying to look modest.

Scarlet translated the conversation for Jem, who didn't bother trying to look modest about his discovery. Then she turned back to her new friends and said casually, "I can't help but notice your clothes." She pointed to Sina's dress. "That must've been a jolly coat."

Sina blushed. "It was yours, wasn't it? I'm sorry," she said. Then she added slyly, "But if it makes it any better, *we* didn't actually steal it." She whistled, and a small black monkey with a kink in his tail and fur that stood up on one side of his head scampered up to them.

"Hey!" Jem cried. "I know him!"

"You!" Scarlet exclaimed. "Little scalawag!" The monkey gave her the same hopeful look that had convinced her to part with her boots to begin with. Scarlet had to laugh. "But wait. You can communicate with this monkey?"

The Islanders nodded. The monkey scrambled up onto Kapu's shoulder and began picking through the boy's hair. Kapu swatted his fingers away.

"You can feel what he's feeling?" she asked.

Sina nodded.

"*And* talk back?"

She nodded again.

"But how?"

Sina shrugged. "We talk to him in our language. He understands."

Scarlet walked in silence for a moment, digesting this. Then she turned to Jem and relayed the information.

Jem jumped at the news. "Then my theory might be right!" he cried. "If the island animals have learned the Islander language, it only makes sense that the pigs learned Old World English! Scarlet, this is huge! It's a groundbreaking discovery!"

Scarlet only nodded. She'd had quite enough groundbreaking discoveries for one day.

When they reached the edge of the clearing, Sina paused, her eyes darting around as if looking for an escape route. But Kapu marched right out of the jungle so his sister had no choice but to follow.

"Captain!" Liam and Gil called as they came running across the grass.

"We were wondering where you were," Liam cried. "We need you to settle an—" He stopped short when he saw the two newcomers. "What the—?"

"Liam and Gil, meet Sina and Kapu," said Scarlet.

"Are they . . . ?" Gil stared down at Kapu, then up at Sina, and his lower lip trembled.

"What's wrong, Gil? You act like you've never seen an Islander before," Jem said, brushing past the boy. "How very Old World of you."

Scarlet grinned. Beside her, Sina whispered something to Kapu.

Within moments, they were surrounded by wide-eyed Lost Souls introducing themselves to the Islanders and apologizing to Jem. Finally, after she and Kapu had been thoroughly overwhelmed with all the new names, Sina pulled Scarlet aside.

"So the pirates know about the treasure?" she asked.

"Well, they know for sure now that it's rubies," Scarlet replied, "but they don't know that they're in the aras' nests."

"You're sure."

"Well, yes." Scarlet looked into the girl's eyes, which had turned wary once again. Kapu joined them, looking puzzled.

"Then why," said Sina, "is one of them here?"

"Huh?"

"One of the pirates," Kapu joined in. "Right there." He pointed behind her.

Scarlet spun around. The rest of the Lost Souls did the same.

"What?" Gil Jenkins cried. "Why are you all looking at me?"

CHAPTER FIFTEEN

Jem had seen Scarlet come close to throttling people before. Like Elmo, the time he dropped his dagger from the crow's nest and it narrowly missed her head. And of course Lucas Lawrence when he defected to the *Dark Ranger* with the treasure map. But judging by the look on her face, he doubted she'd ever wanted to wring a person's neck so badly than she did just then.

Tim must have figured the same.

"Captain, no!" he yelled as she surged through the crowd, straight for Gil Jenkins.

And Gil must have seen it coming, too, for he immediately covered his throat. "They're lying!" he cried. "Whatever they said, it's a lie!"

Jem dove between them just in time, blocking Scarlet's path. "Wait, Captain! At least tell us what's wrong before you kill him."

"Let's let Gil tell us, shall we?" Scarlet ducked past him and grabbed Gil by the collar. "What did you do?" She lifted the boy a few inches off the ground.

Gil squirmed and kicked, but Scarlet held tight. "Erm . . . what'd they say I did?"

Scarlet spoke through clenched teeth. "Gil, have you been meeting with Lucas Lawrence?"

The Lost Souls gasped.

Jem smacked his forehead. "I *knew* something was

going on! I kept seeing him in the jungle by himself!"

Scarlet tightened her grip on Gil's collar. "Tell me."

For a moment Gil looked frightened. Then he pressed his lips together, narrowed his eyes, and said nothing.

"What were you doing out there alone?"

Gil spat out of the corner of his mouth. "Can't a pirate go off by himself to do his business?"

"Not if your business is being a *traitor*!" Jem yelled. He could have kicked himself for not tackling Gil the first time he saw him in the jungle alone.

"Smitty," Scarlet called, "what's the island warrior equivalent of a keelhaul?"

Smitty leaned over her shoulder, grinning wickedly. "I'm glad you asked, Cap'n. I was just going to suggest that very method of torture, reserved for prisoners who've committed the very worst crimes."

"And what would that be?" Scarlet asked without taking her eyes off Gil. He avoided her gaze.

"I call it 'target practice.' It's for the good of Island X, of course. I mean, we have to practice our archery skills before taking aim at the pirates and King's Men. Practice makes perfect, they say."

"Yes, I've heard that, too," said Scarlet.

"So we strap the prisoner to a tree, nice and tight, and put, say, a papaya on his head. Then, all together, we let our arrows fly right at that big, juicy fruit."

Gil's pale face took on a shade of green.

"But, Smit," Scarlet growled, her eyes still on Gil, "the Lost Souls have terrible aim. What if we miss?"

Smitty leaned in closer. "It's a chance we've got

to take, isn't it? But I'm sure the prisoner won't mind losing his nose or maybe an eye or two for the good of Island X." He reached over Scarlet's shoulder to poke Gil Jenkins hard, right between the eyes.

Gil looked as if he might spew. Scarlet lifted him an inch higher. "What. Did. You. Do?"

The boy's face crumpled like a wrinkly piece of fruit. "He lied to me," he muttered.

"Who lied?" asked Jem.

"Lucas," Gil whispered. "I hate him."

"Join the crew." Scarlet dropped Gil onto his rear end but didn't let go of his collar. "Explain yourself."

Gil looked up at Scarlet, then back to the ground. "I . . . I met with Lucas," he said.

"Speak up!" someone called from the back of the group.

"I met with Lucas!" Gil shouted, still not looking up from the ground. A few Lost Souls gasped. Others groaned. "But here's the thing: I wasn't going to. I didn't want any more to do with him than any of you. I *didn't*." Finally he looked up at them. "But none of you would trust me. You didn't let me go on any missions, you gave me the worst jobs, you accused me of stealing when I hadn't done *anything*!" He looked at Jem. "I *didn't* steal your knife, Fitz. And I *was* just doing my business in the jungle the other day. I mean, come on, mate. All we eat is fruit!"

"Oh," was all Jem could think of to say to that.

Gil chewed on his lip and studied his dirty fingernails. "So, since you didn't pick me to go spying, I figured I'd go by myself and maybe discover something that would . . . help us, you know . . . make people respect me."

Jem bit his lip, too. That he could understand.

"And early yesterday morning I decided to go find Uncle Finn and Thomas."

"Uncle Finn and Thomas!" Jem echoed. In all the commotion, he'd completely forgotten about the missing explorers. "Did you really?"

Gil nodded. "But I guess I got too close to the pirates' camp, and a few of 'em found me. Those swabs were threatening to boil me alive, but then Lucas showed up and told them to shove off. Then he said that if I told him what and where the treasure was, he'd give me a sack of doubloons and let me join the *Dark Ranger* pirates and share in the booty."

"Gil!" Scarlet cried. "You didn't!"

"No!" Gil looked up at his captain, tears gathering in his eyes. "I didn't. I said I'd think about it, and he let me go. And I *wouldn't* have told him. But then this morning, everything scuttled again. I wasn't allowed to go spying. Everyone had to know what I was up to, all the time. It's always the same, and it's not fair!"

Jem swallowed, torn between feeling sorry for Gil, ashamed at accusing him without reason, and terrified of what was coming next.

"So I went and told him," Gil finished in a whisper.

Tim and Smitty lunged for the traitor, but Scarlet raised her arm to stop them.

"Wait," she said, still looking down at Gil. "Then what happened?"

Two fat tears rolled down Gil's dirty cheeks. "That biscuit-eater went back on his word. He didn't pay me. And he denied ever saying I could join his crew."

Jem rubbed his forehead, suddenly feeling very tired. The boy sitting cross-legged on the grass before them was a scoundrel, absolutely. But this whole situation might have been avoided if he'd been treated just a little differently—by Scarlet, by Jem, by everyone. He could tell that Scarlet, too, wanted to hold her head in her hands and curse the world. But after a moment she cleared her throat and addressed the crew.

"In case you didn't get that, Lucas now knows what and where the treasure is." The Lost Souls burst into shouts and curses, but she raised a hand. "Quiet, everyone." She turned back to Gil, who was picking his fingernails. "What Gil did was wrong. If we had a long drop here, he'd be cleaning it for eternity. And that would only be the beginning of the punishment." The boy hung his head even lower. "But we'll deal with that later. Right now, we've got an invasion on our hands. Gil, what else can you tell us?"

Gil swallowed. "Well, Lucas did say they'd get the King's Men out of the way before coming for the treasure."

A murmur rippled through the crowd.

"The King's Men? Really?"

Jem noticed a strange look crossing Scarlet's face. "What do you mean, get them out of the way?" she snapped.

Gil shrugged. "Attack them, leave no prisoners—the usual."

"Could that . . . work in our favor?" Jem asked, reasoning that at least it would get one enemy out of the way.

Scarlet ignored him. "When will the pirates attack them?"

"Soon, I guess," said Gil. "Maybe tonight?"

Jem looked up at the early-evening sky. This day already felt like one of the longest of his life, and it was nowhere near over.

"All right, crew," said Scarlet. "You heard him. Gather your weapons. Search for ambush spots. We have to be ready for them and head them off before they get anywhere near the treasure."

"What about Gil?" Smitty pointed at him. "What do we do with him?"

Scarlet looked down at the boy. He raised his eyes to meet hers, then quickly lowered them again. "Well?" she said. "What do you think?"

When he spoke, it was barely more than a whisper. "Just let me be part of the crew."

Scarlet studied him a moment longer, then crouched down so that she and Gil were nose to nose. "If you betray us," she hissed, "I will have your sorry rear end carried off by the stinkiest, hairiest, nastiest wild pigs. See if I don't."

Gil nodded vigorously. "I won't. I promise." He hopped to his feet.

The Lost Souls scurried off every which way. Jem looked around and jumped at the sight of Sina and Kapu behind him. He'd completely forgotten about them.

Scarlet brought the Islanders up to speed in that strange way of communicating they had—a word here, an intense stare there. Jem couldn't begin to understand how she did it. When she'd finished, Sina and Kapu both looked thoroughly overwhelmed.

"Maybe Kapu and I can build the base of a tree house so we'll have a place to ambush them from," Jem suggested.

"Good idea," said Scarlet. But she seemed distracted—as if some animal were trying to get her attention again.

"Captain?"

For a moment she looked at Jem as if she couldn't quite see him. Then she nodded. "Fitz, while you're working on the house . . . I think . . . I also need you to do one more thing."

"What's that?"

She pursed her lips, then puffed out her cheeks, thinking hard. "I . . . I need you to be in charge of the crew. I have to disappear for a bit."

"Scarlet, no!" Jem cried. "Not again! Whatever animal it is, forget it! We need you."

"I know, Fitz. But it's not an animal I'm chasing. It's . . . much more important."

Jem crossed his arms, wondering what could possibly be more important than helping them prepare for a pirate attack.

"Look, I'll tell you everything when I get back. I promise. But for now, you've got to believe me that this is important. I wouldn't think of leaving if it weren't."

Jem bit his lip. "I don't know," he said, remembering

his attempts at leading. "The crew doesn't listen to me. I mean, I'm not . . . like you."

"Course you're not like me, Fitz. You're you. That doesn't mean you can't take charge when I'm gone."

Jem wasn't convinced. "I'd like to try, but—"

"But nothing," Scarlet interjected. "You've been doing a jolly job lately. No, I mean it, you *have*. You've got a good head, mate."

"An Old World head."

"Well, yes. And you've used it to solve some big, important mysteries. We need that Old World head of yours."

It was the only time he'd ever heard her compliment something Old World. It gave him hope. "Really?"

"Captain's honor." She crossed her heart. "Now look, I'll be back as soon as I can."

"All right." Jem nodded. "I don't understand what's going on . . . but I trust you." Then he straightened and saluted. "Good luck, Captain."

She saluted back, spoke quickly with the Islanders, and had begun to turn away when Sina grabbed her hand and shook it hard. It was an odd thing to do, Jem thought, but he reasoned that the Islanders weren't familiar with Old World customs. And, anyway, he had more important things to think about. Like his captain taking off to who-knew-where and leaving him in charge of the Lost Souls.

CHAPTER SIXTEEN

Jem breathed slowly to calm his nerves. The pirates were going to attack—by morning at the latest. And he was in charge.

I'm in charge, he told himself. Then he said it out loud to the Islanders. "I'm in charge."

Kapu nodded as if he understood. He looked expectantly at Jem.

"Right. So what do I do now?" Jem tapped his foot on the grass. What needed to be done first? He looked around the clearing at the long shadows cast by the fading light of day.

The answer was obvious. In fact, it stood right beside him.

Sina looked downright upset. She was whispering to her brother, waving her hands and making her bracelets dance on her wrists. While Jem obviously didn't know a word of the language Scarlet was relearning, he could tell Sina was saying something like "Let's get the flotsam out of here!"

Kapu tugged on his sister's hand, but she folded her arms across her chest and issued a command that sounded frighteningly similar to one of Scarlet's. Jem had to do something before Sina scooped up Kapu and made a dash for the jungle.

"Please wait," he said. "We need your help. You can

show me how to build a tree house." He added as many hand gestures as he could to get the point across.

Kapu nodded. Sina shook her head.

"Blast," Jem muttered. Not that he could blame her for wanting to go. She'd witnessed an incredible tragedy thanks to the Old Worlders. Why would she stick around to meet them again, or let them get near her brother?

But he couldn't just let them leave. The Lost Souls needed all the help they could get.

Once again he looked around. The crew was scurrying about, directionless. Edwin dropped the lantern he was lighting and would have started a fire if a few others hadn't stomped it out. Monty yelled at him, and the two started to quarrel. Gil wandered with his hands in his pockets, looking lost. Smitty stood off to one side, letting arrows fly every which way from his bow. Ronagh shrieked and covered her head when one swerved her way.

"That's it!" Jem snapped his fingers. And he turned and beckoned to the Islanders. "Please follow me. Just this once."

Sina sighed and grumbled something to her brother, who grasped her wrist and pulled her after Jem.

He led them across the clearing, weaving through the chaos. Then he stopped, touched Sina on the shoulder, and pointed at Smitty, who was stringing another crooked arrow into his bow, tongue clamped between his teeth.

Sina watched for only a split second before crying out in horror. Her long legs broke into a sprint, and she grabbed Smitty's bow before he could let another arrow fly.

"Yes!" Jem whispered. He'd figured Sina wouldn't be able to stand back and witness such a disaster.

The girl shook her head at Smitty, and he, openmouthed, lowered his weapon. Then she plucked it from his hands and examined its design. She rolled her eyes and said something that probably amounted to "Blimey, I've got a lot of work to do."

Jem and Kapu grinned at each other while Sina drew out her own weapon and handed it to Smitty, adjusting his stance so that he stood square on both feet. Smitty shut his mouth and concentrated on the lesson.

"Excellent," said Jem, turning to Kapu. "Now you and I will go work on the tree house." He pointed in the direction of his unfinished work, and Kapu hopped up and down, impatient. "Let's go!"

They scampered back across the clearing, skirting a dozen or so Lost Souls clustered in the center. Jem was about to dash right on past when he heard Tim's voice. "We've got no ship. We can't use our cloaks as disguises. How are we going to fight them?"

"Scurvy." Jem slowed to a jog and motioned for Kapu to wait.

"The legend of the Lost Souls used to protect us, but now everyone knows we're just children." Tim's voice wavered as he spoke.

"Even the pigs won't help us now," Sam added.

Jem thought back to what Scarlet had told him: That he had succeeded by using his own strengths here on Island X. So if *he* could do it . . .

"On the *Hop* we had it all figured out. We had everything we needed to take on the bad guys."

Jem opened his mouth to interject, but another Lost Soul cut in.

"Island X is totally different. What've we got here?"

"But—" Jem began.

"If we were on the *Hop* we might stand a—"

"All right, that's enough!" Jem shouted. Over a dozen faces turned toward him, surprised. "Listen to yourselves! So what if you're not on the *Hop* right now? You're no different, any one of you, than you were last month, or the month before that. You've still got all the skills you had at home. Those don't just disappear in the jungle."

He stopped to take a breath and was alarmed to find them all listening to him. So he continued. "You've got to take your Lost Soul skills and talents and combine them with what you've learned on Island X."

"Sounds jolly," someone called from the back of the group. "But how?"

"Well . . ." Jem thought for a moment. "Take Elmo, for one. He's a wicked climber. Scales the mast to the crow's nest in less than a minute, right?"

"Forty-three seconds, actually," Elmo said, blushing.

"So here he can climb trees instead of masts. He can hide and tell us when the pirates are approaching. We've got lots of good climbers, so we can have lots of lookouts."

A few Lost Souls murmured that this was true.

"What else?" someone asked.

"Oh, blimey," Jem said under his breath, racking his brain for answers. "How about—"

"Bull's-eye!" A cry interrupted him. The Lost Souls turned to see Smitty with his fists in the air, triumphant.

"Didja see that?" He pointed to an arrow lodged in a tree some twenty yards away. "A perfect shot! Sina taught me, just like that!" And Smitty turned to his teacher with a look of pure adoration.

"Archery!" Jem cried. "Those of you who have good aim'll pick it up fast. Sina'll show you!"

The Lost Souls began to whisper among themselves.

"Charlie, that's you. You've got good aim."

"Well, that's true."

"Come on, what else are you good at?" Jem pressed.

"How about rope tying?" someone else suggested.

"The rope tiers could make a trap!" Monty shouted. "When a pirate steps in it, he'll get strung up!"

"Hey!" Tim cried suddenly. "I can do that! I know just the knot!"

"I'll help!"

The crowd broke off into smaller groups. Some headed toward Smitty and Sina. Others ran off to find rope for their trap. Jem couldn't help but gape at his own success. By giving the Lost Souls reason to believe in themselves, he'd convinced them that they could protect the island.

"Um, Jem," a small, gruff voice spoke up behind him. Jem turned to see Gil Jenkins, hands still stuffed in his trouser pockets. The boy glanced up at him, then down at the ground. "Anything . . . I can do?"

Jem regarded him for a moment, wondering when Gil had last felt important—like he was really good at something. He'd been a lowly cabin boy before becoming Lucas Lawrence's sidekick, so it had probably been ages.

Jem thought for a moment. "Well," he said finally, "you've always been good with a dagger, Gil. Why don't you take yours and get Sina to show you how to carve arrows? I bet you'd be good at that."

At first Gil looked as if he wasn't sure whether to believe Jem. Then, finally, he nodded. "I think I could do that."

"Course you could. You'll be a real fletcher."

"A what now?"

Jem sighed. "A person who makes arrows. Go on."

Gil mouthed the word *fletcher* to himself, then fished his dagger out of his boot and trotted off.

Finally Jem turned to Kapu. "Whew. That's done. Now it's just you and me and the tree house."

But on the way, they passed Uncle Finn's and Thomas's piles of belongings, and Jem stopped. Once again he'd forgotten about the explorers, and the realization filled him with a dreadful certainty. There was no way they'd been gone this long looking for plants. Uncle Finn and Thomas had met with foul play—and Jem was fairly certain he knew who to blame.

Kapu tugged on Jem's sleeve.

"It's my uncle," Jem explained, not caring if Kapu could understand him. "I just don't know what to do."

Kapu tugged again, and Jem looked down at him. The boy wore an impatient look—a look that told Jem exactly what he had to do. The only thing he *could* do, in fact.

Defeat the pirates.

CHAPTER SEVENTEEN

As she tore through the trees once again, Scarlet wondered how many times she'd run this route in the last few days. It felt like hundreds. In fact, she realized after a while, despite the growing darkness, she now recognized nearly every turn and tree she passed. She was steering herself rather than relying on the island. And what's more, thanks to some nice new calluses, she barely felt the twigs and burrs underfoot.

"Well, really, who needs boots?" she puffed as she ran. "Or a map for that matter." She ducked a split second before knocking her head on an overhanging branch. "But a lantern. Now that'd be nice."

Still, she had something even better tucked inside her trouser pocket. It had taken her a moment to recognize it when Sina had pressed it into her hand before she left. *How did Sina know?* Scarlet wondered.

The King's Men were beginning to light their own lamps, giving the tents a warm glow. Once again Scarlet crouched in the bushes and picked up a stone. She hesitated before throwing it, asking herself one more time if she'd made the right decision. Part of her still couldn't believe she'd left her crew at such an important time. But a larger part of her knew she'd done what she had to do.

She nailed the admiral's tent with her stone. "Come on," she whispered. "Come on, it's important."

She had to throw three before a shadow finally stirred inside the tent. The admiral stepped out hesitantly, as if he feared the awful memories she might inflict on him this time.

She didn't give him a chance to speak. "Clearing. Right now," she whispered, and darted off.

She waited there, arms folded across her chest, tapping a bare foot on the grass. He appeared minutes later, approaching slowly with a lantern at his side. And looking very, very tired.

"Scarlet, this had better be important. We're moving out tomorrow morning, and I have a lot to do—"

"I know, Father. I don't have much time, either. The pirates are going to attack your camp. Tonight."

Admiral McCray started. "What? How do you know?"

"It's a long story."

He settled his fists on his hips.

She sighed. "All right, but I have to make it quick. See, one of my crew—Lucas Lawrence—defected to the *Dark Ranger* about a month ago, and he's been using another one of my mates—Gil Jenkins—to spy on us. So Gil—he's a bit of a twit, but I do think he means well— gave away some very, *very* important information that's booted the pirates into action. They want to get your men out of the way before heading our way. So you see why I'm in a bit of a hurry."

Admiral McCray shook his head. "Wait! Why do these pirates need to do away with us first? What do they want from you?"

"That's a long story, too. Maybe another—"

"Now."

She debated for a long moment but couldn't think of another way to get him to believe her. So she shut her eyes and silently asked Island X for forgiveness. "The treasure," she said very softly.

"Treasure?"

She opened her eyes and nodded. "The one we're guarding. The rubies."

"Rubies?"

"Well, it's more than that, really, but the rubies are what everyone else considers—"

"More than that?"

"Father, this might go faster if you stopped repeating everything I say."

He shook his head again. "Let me get this straight. You, my daughter, are protecting a treasure—rubies, among other things—on this island. The pirates know about it, and they're going to attack you. But first they've got to get my men out of the way."

"Yes, that basically sums it up."

He held up the lantern and looked at her closely, as if to determine whether she was lying. "So this is what your crew does?"

Scarlet shrugged. "Not usually. But that's another story altogether. Right now you need to get your men ready for an attack. The pirates'll probably be here soon."

He heaved an enormous sigh. "Fine. Fine. I'll tell the men. We'll stage a counterattack, take prisoners, and be off tomorrow morning. And you'll meet me here."

Scarlet looked up. "Tomorrow? No. I told you, Father. I can't go with you."

His eyes narrowed. "Scarlet. I'm sure you feel you have to stay and protect this . . . this treasure. But it's not worth it. A mountain of rubies wouldn't be worth it."

"It's not just about the rubies," she insisted. "The entire island needs protecting—the aras, the trees, the pigs, and . . . and . . ." She gulped. "The Islanders."

"The who?"

She spoke slowly, hoping once again she'd made the right decision. "That's why I asked you to teach me our old language yesterday. Two Islander children survived the fever, and now they're helping us protect the treasure. At least, I hope they'll stay and help . . ."

"Islanders?" Her father looked positively stunned.

"Islanders," said Scarlet. "I thought you should know because . . . well, it gives us another reason for being here and protecting the island. It's for them, too." She bit her lip. "I can't leave."

After a long silence, she spoke again. "I have to go now, Father. And so do you. The pirates will be coming soon."

Her father stood so still that she might have mistaken him for a statue.

"I have to go," she said again. "Take care of yourself."

And she extended a hand, just as Sina had done to her earlier. When she pressed Sina's gift into his hand, his mouth opened in confusion. But before he could say anything, she was off again.

The jungle reverberated with nocturnal noises: buzzing insects, throaty toads, hissing . . . something-or-others. Scarlet tried not to think about all the strange creatures hanging over her head or slithering around her bare feet. The sky was now thoroughly dark, so she had to rely on her senses and memory to get back to the clearing.

She was deep in concentration when she heard a noise that most definitely didn't belong to any insect, frog, or reptile. She paused and held her breath, hoping her ears had played a trick on her. Or perhaps some nocturnal bird had gotten very good at imitating—

"Would ye get off me foot, ye oaf?"

Scarlet spun around and saw them, not twenty yards to her left. A very dim lantern illuminated their shadows, but Scarlet didn't need another speck of light to know with all certainty that these were the *Dark Ranger* pirates.

"Sorry. Didn't see ye there."

"Shut up, both of ye!"

What are they doing? she wondered. They've gone right past the King's Men's camp. Are they lost? Or are they . . . oh *no*.

Scarlet inched toward their light with a very bad feeling about what she was about to find.

The entire *Dark Ranger* crew clustered around a few lanterns. Voices drifted up from the middle, and Scarlet knew she'd have to get closer to hear what they were saying. She looked around and found the perfect tree, with long branches leaning out over the pirates' huddle. She scaled it as quietly as she could, holding her breath when a few leaves drifted down, narrowly missing a pirate's bare head. Scarlet lay on her stomach on the overhanging branch and pulled herself along it until she had the perfect view of the events unfolding below.

Captain Wallace stood in the center of the huddle with Pete and Lucas behind him. Every now and then one of his right-hand men would stick out his tongue or cross his eyes at the other behind the captain's back.

"Oh, I know they're only children," the captain was saying, "but you never know what kind of beast will burst out of the trees to protect them. So be ready. Kill anything in your path."

Blast, thought Scarlet. *They* are *coming for us*. But what about the King's Men? Weren't they supposed to be first?

"Think they know we're comin'?" one pirate asked.

Captain Wallace turned to Lucas for the answer. Unfortunately, he turned just in time to see Lucas pulling his lips apart with his fingers to bare all his teeth at Pete. The captain jumped at the sight of Lucas's yellow teeth, and Lucas snapped his mouth shut. Pete grinned.

"Pay attention, stupid," the captain snarled. "Do the Lost Souls know we're coming?"

Lucas cleared his throat. "I told Gil we'd raid the King's Men's camp first. So they won't be expecting us yet, anyway. We'll take 'em by surprise."

Now it was Scarlet's turn to snarl. What she would give for a big, long stick to bean him with. The King's Men weren't going to be attacked after all—at least, not until after the pirates had the treasure. And here she was, so far from her crew. Cursed Lucas Lawrence!

"And you think the child believed you?" Pete challenged him.

Lucas grinned. "Gil was stupid enough to trust me in the first place. And stupid enough not to realize that we had what he was looking for."

Captain Wallace looked at Lucas like a proud father. "Good work, boy."

Lucas puffed out his chest and shouted, "Bring forth the prisoners!"

The captain cackled, then stopped. "Wait, that's my line."

The crowd parted, and two men were shoved into the center. One was very tall with enormous shoulders, and the other much shorter and rounder.

"Uncle Finn and Thomas!" Scarlet hissed, then bit her knuckles. She almost hadn't recognized them because . . . she squinted into the lantern light. Because both men had sprouted abundant heads of hair! Thomas's was long and brown and silky, while Uncle Finn had thick, unruly curls. "Sink me!" Scarlet whispered. "The cure for andro-alo-whatsit!"

Their hands and feet were bound, and each was gagged with a dirty handkerchief. Pirates walked behind them, daring them to run with the prick points of their cutlasses.

"If the Lost Souls make one false move, the hostages will die!" Lucas yelled. The pirates cheered.

"Stop that! You're stealing all the good lines!" Captain Wallace whined.

Scarlet took that as her cue to slip back down to the ground. This was no time to sit and watch. She had to get home and prepare her crew for battle.

She'd expected to find them all asleep when she burst out of the jungle and into the clearing. It was, after all, the middle of the night. But instead she found them sitting near the pool, whittling arrows and stringing bows by the light of a few jars of fireflies.

"Scarlet!" Ronagh cried when she saw her captain approaching. "She's back!"

The other Lost Souls turned to greet her as well, but without the usual panic she'd lately come to expect. They looked more determined and focused than they had since leaving the *Hop*.

Scarlet found Jem at the center of the crowd with Sina and Kapu on either side of him. He grinned at her. Good old Fitz! She knew he could do it.

"Where were you?" Elmo asked when Scarlet reached them.

She paused for a moment, then decided she'd tell them the whole truth later. "I was . . . out scouting. And I found the *Dark Ranger* pirates."

"Attacking the King's Men?" Tim asked.

Scarlet shook her head. "They aren't attacking them first after all. Lucas told Gil that to make us think we had time to spare."

"What?" Gil cried. "Why that big—"

"Wait. It gets worse," said Scarlet. "Not only are they on their way here, they've got hostages."

"Hostages?"

Jem jumped to his feet. "Uncle Finn!"

"And Thomas!" Smitty leaped up beside him.

Scarlet nodded grimly. "So now we've got to protect the treasure and fight off the pirates without putting Uncle Finn and Thomas in any more danger."

"But Thomas is a giant," said Smitty. "He can fight back."

"I don't know if even Thomas can take on forty pirates at once," said Scarlet. "He needs our help."

"Blimey," Jem said shakily. Then he cleared his throat. "Well, at least we're prepared. Sina's been teaching archery, and a bunch of us made really good bows and arrows. And other people set traps around the edge of the clearing. Kapu and I tried to build the tree house, but it got dark before we could finish it. So it's just a platform, and I'm not sure how sturdy—"

"I bet it's great, Fitz. Excellent work. So we're ready?"

"Ready as we'll ever be," Jem replied. "I even went and spoke to the smelly wild pig chief—"

"You did? You asked him for help?" Scarlet could only imagine how badly that conversation had gone.

Jem shook his head. "Just to advise him to hide his band and tell him that we've got this all under control."

Scarlet marveled at Jem's new confidence. She hoped he was right.

"We also decided we don't really need elaborate costumes," Smitty added, stealing a glance at Sina. He held up the leafy hat he'd been weaving. "Just some simple camouflage will do."

"She laughed at the Deadly Parrot of Death," Ronagh whispered to Scarlet.

Despite their situation, Scarlet grinned. "Camouflage," she said. "Always a good idea. Too bad we can't use it to protect the . . ." Her voice trailed off as an idea suddenly popped into her mind. She stared at Smitty's handiwork, wondering if she'd gone completely loony or if it just might work.

"Captain?" Jem said. "What's up?"

"I think . . . I've got an idea," Scarlet said. "It's worth a shot. We've only got a few minutes. Fitz, get those bromeli-whatsit samples from Uncle Finn's pile. Not the ones that erased Thomas's memory. Then meet me under the aras' nests."

"Okay." Jem sounded uncertain.

Scarlet gestured for Sina and Kapu to come with her. "The rest of you, get ready. The pirates'll come from that way." She jerked her thumb over her shoulder.

Jem ran off across the clearing, and Sina and Kapu followed her toward the aras.

"If this works," Scarlet told them, "it could save the treasure. Maybe even all of Island X!" She explained the plan, then instructed Kapu to fetch the stilts he'd brought. Then Jem arrived with the plant samples.

"You sure about this?" he asked.

"Not a bit," Scarlet said. "But sometimes it's the crazy ideas that work best."

Jem saluted and ran back to the clearing.

Scarlet scrambled up the closest tree until she reached the spot where she usually sat to watch the birds. None of the feathered bodies moved, but she could tell they were aware of her presence. And that they trusted her.

"Let's hope this works," she muttered, then she called upon all the Islander words she'd learned that day, hoping the aras wouldn't be too confused if she forgot a few.

She began to explain the plan: "Now this is very important. My friends are going to visit each of your nests and give you a snack. And while you eat, they're going to redecorate your nests. Trust them, and no biting. We're doing this to keep you safe."

She signaled to Sina and Kapu on their stilts, and the pair moved in closer, handing out bromeliad snacks and moving the rubies inside each nest. The birds looked baffled but pleased with the late-night snack.

Once they were finished, the trio met on the jungle floor. Scarlet gave each of her friends a hug and told them they were brilliant.

"How soon will it work?" Sina asked.

Scarlet looked over her shoulder at the rookery, then to the east where the sky was growing light. "No idea. Fingers crossed for right away."

And then she felt a tremble deep inside her, and although she couldn't tell which animal or reptile or insect or Islander it came from, she knew without a doubt what it meant.

CHAPTER EIGHTEEN

Tim snuffed out their lantern, leaving the Lost Souls in the half darkness of the hour before dawn. Scarlet stuck a fist in the middle of their huddle, and two dozen fists piled on top of it.

"No prey, no pay, mateys."

"No prey, no pay."

"And may you die peacefully rather than be tossed in the Boiling Lake by that dog Lucas."

"Die peacefully!"

"Everybody in their places. And be quiet!"

The Lost Souls and Islanders dove every which way into the jungle, rustled around for a few moments, then settled into perfect stillness. From her perch in a tree, Scarlet could make out Liam and Ronagh armed with slingshots below, and Smitty and Sina behind them, bows and arrows at the ready. The Islander girl looked up and gave her a nervous smile, and Scarlet mouthed a heartfelt thank-you. Then she closed her eyes and tuned in to Island X's wildlife. The creatures were obviously upset. She guessed that meant the pirates were making their way across the clearing. Her heart began to thump. What if the bromeliad needed more time?

But there was no time to wonder, for now she could hear and see them herself. The Dread Pirate Captain Wallace Hammerstein-Jones walked out front, sniffling as though he had a runny nose. Then came Lucas, tromping in his big boots. Then Pete, shuffling reluctantly. And finally forty or so more pirates.

As they neared the edge of the clearing, just to the left of the Lost Souls' hiding spot, Lucas paused and turned. "Would you quit stepping on my heels?" he hissed.

"Oh, was I?" an innocent-sounding Pete answered. "I had no idea. How rude of me."

"Shut up, you twits." The captain wiped his nose on his sleeve. "Where are those little brats? You don't suppose they left?"

"No way," said Lucas. "They've got to be hiding."

"They could be anywheres!" a pirate piped up from the rear of the group. His mates cast fearful glances up at the trees.

"They're only children, you lily-livers," Captain Wallace snapped. "Lucas, which way to the treasure?"

"Dead ahead, Cap'n." Lucas peered at the map. "Should be just in these trees."

Scarlet held her breath as they waded into the bushes, passing the Lost Souls on the right. *Stay together now,* she warned the pirates silently. *If one of you swabs strays this way, we're all fish food.*

Fortunately, the pirates looked too frightened to leave their pack. A few days on Island X had apparently done nothing to ease their fear of the jungle.

Scarlet turned her head slowly, trying to spot the aras behind her. She couldn't see anything, and she prayed that this meant the bromeliad had taken effect. She also prayed that Sina and Kapu hadn't overlooked a single ruby. Just one glint of red in the morning light would spell the end of them, and the end of Island X as they knew it.

"Um, Cap'n," Lucas spoke up after a few minutes. "I . . . think we're here."

"Here?" Captain Wallace stopped and looked around. "Where?"

"Well, the map says the treasure's"—he spread his big arms—"right here."

Scarlet's heart began to pound. Lucas, Pete, and Captain Wallace were standing right in front of the ara rookery. She stared at it until she saw a green head pop up, then duck back into its nest. The bromeliad had taken effect!

Please don't move, she tried to tell the aras. *Don't even rustle a feather. And for goodness' sake don't touch those rubies!*

"I don't see anything," one pirate commented. "'Cept a few green parroty-things up there."

"Me neither," said another. "Sure this is the right place?"

"Let me see that map." Pete reached for the paper, but Lucas held it away from him. "Oh, give it to someone who can actually read it, you numskull!"

Scarlet signaled to the ground crew to start surrounding the pirates while they were distracted. She inched forward on her branch for a better view and spotted a familiar figure—enormous, like Thomas, but with that radiant head of hair. Beside him, Uncle Finn stared at the ground. Both men were still gagged with handkerchiefs, their hands bound behind their backs.

She must have moved too quickly, for suddenly Thomas looked up and saw her. Startled, he quickly looked away, but not before his captor noticed. The extraordinarily hairy pirate behind him had followed Thomas's gaze to Scarlet's tree and was now staring right at her. After a moment's pause, he jumped as if he'd just realized that she wasn't, in fact, a very large monkey.

"Here we go," Scarlet muttered. Before the pirate could shout to his mates, she raised two fingers to her lips and blasted a signal.

The Lost Souls burst out of their hiding places, their hollers startling the pirates so badly that a few actually dropped their cutlasses and ran. The few dozen remaining fumbled for their weapons, only to find themselves ambushed by arrows and stones from all sides. Sina and Smitty each pinned two pirates to the same big tree. Liam and Ronagh whipped rocks at Uncle Finn's and Thomas's captors until they covered their heads and ran off, whimpering.

Scarlet jumped down from her perch and slashed the ropes that bound the captives' hands. The men wasted no time ripping off their gags.

"Oh no ye don't!" A pirate with a face full of scars was running straight for them, cutlass drawn.

"Uncle Finn!" Jem yelled. He pulled something out of his pocket and tossed it to his uncle, who stared at it for a second before his face lit up.

"Cover your ears!" Uncle Finn ordered, then raised the pipe to his lips and blew with all his might.

Scarlet managed to cover her ears just in time, but Scarface and about five of his comrades weren't so lucky. Instantly deafened, they keeled over, giving Thomas a chance to sweep them all up under his arm and toss them into the clearing. Tim, Edwin, and Emmett chased a half dozen more after him, cracking vine-whips above their heads. Shouts thundered and cutlasses clanged throughout the jungle.

"I think we're driving them back!" Monty shouted above the clamor.

"Keep it up, crew!" Scarlet yelled. Then out of the corner of her eye she saw a figure bounding across the clearing toward them. "Some are coming back! There's one . . . wait a minute." She turned for a good look at the figure, then gasped. This was no pirate. This was a man in blue and brass.

"Father!"

A pirate lunged toward her, but she booted him in the knee and hurdled him as he fell. Then she ran to meet the admiral.

"Scarlet!" he cried, his eyes wild and bright. "Are you all right?"

"Of course! We're driving them back!" She paused to wipe a stream of sweat from her forehead.

"When they didn't attack us, I knew something was wrong. I—"

"Arrrgh!" The pirate Scarlet had kicked half ran, half limped toward them, cutlass raised.

"Oh, honestly." Scarlet drew her own slingshot and pelted him in the knuckle with a stone, forcing him to drop his weapon. Then she shot another right at his ear, and he keeled over again, trying to clutch his knee, ear, and left hand all at once.

Admiral McCray looked down at his daughter as if seeing her for the first time. "So *this* is what your crew does?"

Scarlet grinned. "This is what we do best."

"Captain, what's going on?" Jem cried, pointing at Admiral McCray.

"It's all right," Scarlet yelled back. "He's on our side. He's here to help. Right, Father?"

"Father?" Jem cried. "Like, yours?"

"Bit of a long story, Fitz. Maybe later?" She turned back to the admiral. "You *are* here to help, aren't you?"

He looked around at the battle scene, then nodded. "You bet I am!" he cried, drawing his broadsword. And he leaped at the nearest pirate, who responded by punching him in the chest.

"Hey!" Scarlet yelled. But to her surprise, it was the pirate and not the admiral who cried out in pain. Scarlet's father watched him keel over, then patted his breast pocket and winked at Scarlet. He proceeded to charge a nearby group of three, hollering battle cries and curses that made Smitty look away from his next target and whistle.

"Now that's an admirable admiral," the boy quipped.

"That," Scarlet replied, "is my father."

"Your *what*?"

"Later! Let's drive these pirates home!"

The pirates were now fleeing across the clearing,

chased by arrows, stones, and grinning island warriors. The Lost Souls followed them over the grass, around the pool, and straight to the mouth of the trail.

Then Captain Wallace stopped and wiped his nose on his sleeve. "What . . . what *is* this?" he whined. "They're children! They can't chase us off! We were right there, at the treasure!"

"Captain, there's no treasure!" Pete yelled back. "That stupid boy led us astray."

"But the stories—" the captain said.

"Birds hiding rubies? Captain, that's absurd! It's—"

But Pete didn't get to finish, for the rope trap in which he and Captain Wallace had been standing clamped tight around their legs, and before they could even yelp, they'd been strung up in a tree.

Scarlet cheered. Tim had sneaked in and sprung the trap while the pirates were arguing. It was brilliant! It was—

"McCray!"

It was Lucas Lawrence, cutlass drawn, looking none too pleased at being foiled in his attempt to steal the treasure.

The floor of Jem's tree house hung a few feet above Scarlet's head. Just before Lucas could reach her, she clambered up onto it.

"Think you're safe up there?" Lucas growled. "You have no idea what's coming to you." He clamped his cutlass between his teeth, grasped a low branch, and followed her up.

"Oh, I know what's coming to me," Scarlet retorted.

"Even if I didn't have eyes I could smell you."

There was no time to congratulate herself on the excellent comeback. In a moment, they'd both be standing on a very small platform with nothing to do but fight. Scarlet gulped. She'd been in this situation before. But this time, there were no pigs to save her.

Below, Jem came running toward the tree. "Stop! Stop!"

Lucas shoved him away and pulled himself up onto the platform.

"I don't think it's . . ." Scarlet heard Jem say. "Oh, scurvy."

Lucas stood and plucked his cutlass from his teeth. He gave Scarlet a wicked smirk. "This is it, McCray. The moment we've all been waiting for."

Then she heard the first snap. Realizing what was about to happen, she spotted a vine hanging nearby that just might hold her.

When the platform broke, splintering into a hundred pieces, she leaped for that vine.

Lucas tumbled to the jungle floor, knocking himself clean out of consciousness.

"HURRAY!" the Lost Souls below yelled as their captain swung down to meet them.

"Brilliant, Cap'n!" Smitty yelled. "A real island warrior, you are."

Scarlet bent double for a moment to slow her heartbeats and her breath. Finally she looked up and shook her head.

"A real Lost Soul."

CHAPTER NINETEEN

"Lost Soul? As in the Ship of Lost Souls? *That's* what your crew does?"

"Um. Well . . ."

Admiral McCray looked around at the Lost Souls, who were staring back at him equally bewildered. "Little ghouls, all dressed in black," he murmured. "I can't believe it."

"Captain," Tim whispered, "how do you know he . . . I mean, he *is* a King's Man and all."

"I know." Scarlet turned to her crew. "But he won't tell. Right, Father?"

He looked at the Lost Souls, then at the clearing beyond. "I won't tell a soul," he said.

Looking up at his messy hair and bright eyes, Scarlet doubted he'd ever said anything so true. The stern admiral was fading right before her eyes.

"The pirates won't get far," he continued. "My men are waiting a few hundred yards away in the trees. And no," he added as Tim opened his mouth, "I didn't tell them anything. I ordered them to lead me to the place where they killed the pig and stay put until I said so. Capturing any pirates who came their way, of course."

Scarlet marveled at how the jagged lines on her father's face had disappeared. She wanted desperately to talk to him alone, but there would be time for that later.

Right now, they had a few more pirates to deal with.

She turned to Lucas Lawrence, still unconscious on the jungle floor. Jem stood beside him. "I'm not sure how to feel about this shoddy construction job." He kicked a broken stick.

Scarlet punched him lightly in the shoulder. "Are you kidding, Fitz? Your tree house saved us all, just like you wanted it to. Well, all right, maybe not *just* like you wanted it to."

Jem laughed. "So what should we do with him?"

"And those two?" Ronagh pointed to Captain Wallace and Iron "Pete" Morgan, who were hanging upside-down from a nearby tree. The captain was complaining that the rope was chafing his ankles, while Pete sighed, holding his head in his hands.

"Hmm." Scarlet looked around at her crew, her father, Thomas, and Uncle Finn. Her eyes lingered on the last two. Then she cried, "I've got it! We'll feed them that bromeliad!"

"I dunno," said Thomas. "Neither of them's got andro . . . alo . . . they've both got lots of hair."

Scarlet shook her head. "The other one."

"Really? I don't think green really suits either of 'em," Smitty mused.

Scarlet rolled her eyes. "The *other* one. The one that'll erase their memories."

"Jolly!" said Jem. "Uncle Finn and I will go get some. Nice hair, by the way," he added to his uncle.

"You like it?" Uncle Finn touched his curly mane. "It's not too much?"

Jem grinned. "Not at all. It suits you. And, Uncle Finn, I've got to tell you about my new theory. It might sound crazy, but I think it's sound. It has to do with animals learning languages, see . . ." His voice trailed off as they walked away.

Most of the other Lost Souls busied themselves tying up Lucas and lowering Captain Wallace and Pete from the tree so they could tie them up tighter.

Scarlet watched for a moment, then turned to her father.

"Thank you," she said at the same time he said, "I'm sorry."

"Don't—" she began, but he shook his head.

"I've been a terrible father, too consumed by my own grief and anger to focus on the one thing that mattered—you. I left you with that old woman, thinking she couldn't possibly be a worse caregiver than me. At that point, I thought life couldn't get any worse. And then you disappeared. I searched for you for *three years*, Scarlet. Three years of anguish. Three years of wondering if you'd be around every corner I turned."

Scarlet nodded, remembering her time with Scary Mary, when every footstep on the stairs held the possibility of being her father's.

"And then," he continued, "as soon as I gave up, there you were. The spitting image of your mother. Except dirtier." He reached out and tugged on a lock of her hair.

"Really?" Scarlet blinked hard.

"When you got angry the other day, I saw her right before me, in you. And I began to remember what we'd been through and . . . I was terrified. I didn't think I could handle the memories. But then . . ." He reached into his breast pocket and pulled out the wooden star. The one he'd carved for Scarlet many years ago. The one Sina had somehow saved and handed to Scarlet the day before. The one Scarlet had passed on to her father in hopes that he'd remember.

"I did," he said simply.

Scarlet slipped her hand into his. "Come on." She led him a short ways off, where Sina and Kapu stood watching. When he saw them, the admiral stopped and drew a breath.

"Thank you," Scarlet said to them through words and thoughts. "We couldn't have done that without you."

Sina and Kapu nodded without taking their eyes off the King's Man before them.

Finally, Sina spoke up. "I remember you," she told Admiral McCray in her language.

For a moment he said nothing. Scarlet felt his hand tighten and wondered if it would be too much for him—if it might make him run away.

But finally he nodded. "I remember, too. You and Scarlet were inseparable."

Scarlet's jaw dropped. Not so much because of what he'd said—she had suspected that when Sina had slipped her the wooden star—but because of how he'd said it. In the Islander language.

She marveled at him for a moment, then turned to Sina. "Did you know we were friends?"

Sina bit her lip. "I wasn't sure at first. You look

different now." She pointed at Scarlet's shirt and trousers, then grinned. "But you still play a mean game of *tapo*. So I figured it out."

"*Tapo,*" Admiral McCray murmured. "Looks like I have a lot to catch up on."

Scarlet looked up at him. "But you're going away . . . aren't you?"

He laid a hand on her head. "It occurred to me, when I saw you and your crew in this place I'd forgotten all about, that the Old World doesn't need me. If you're here, and you're here, too"—he nodded to Sina and Kapu—"then I need to make sure that they"—he nodded toward the trees, where his men were capturing pirates as they spoke—"don't come anywhere near this place. That"—he smiled—"will be my new job."

"A renegade King's Man!" Scarlet exclaimed, wrapping her arms around his waist. "Infiltrating the enemies from within!" She couldn't wait to tell the crew.

Jem and Uncle Finn soon returned with the plant samples and got to work stuffing them into the captives' mouths. Lucas was just beginning to wake up and find himself cocooned in rope.

"Give 'em lots of that bromely-stuff," Smitty crowed. "Let's make sure they forget all about Island X. And about the Lost Souls!"

Uncle Finn shook his curly mane and said, "Unfortunately, I can't guarantee they'll forget everything forever. We haven't tested this specimen adequately. But"—he pushed a big leaf into Captain Wallace's mouth—"we'll do our very best."

"Now what?" Elmo yelled.

"I say we go to the *Hop*!" Scarlet said. "We'll dump these swabs on the Island of Vengeful Vegetation and do a supply run in Jamestown while we're out."

"Finally!" Tim yelled. "A trip to the ship!"

"And I'll move my men and the rest of the *Dark Ranger* pirates out of here," said Admiral McCray.

"But you'll be back?" Scarlet asked.

"Of course," he answered. "As soon as I spread all kinds of rumors about the horrors on this island and the small but fierce creatures that live here."

The Lost Souls laughed.

"We'll stay and keep watch," Sina said, and Kapu nodded.

"Actually," Gil Jenkins spoke up, "I think I might stay. I'm thinking about planting a garden. For . . . you know . . . a bit of variety."

Scarlet smiled at him. "Sounds like a perfect job. Sina and Kapu'll teach you." Then she turned to the rest of her crew. "To the *Hop* then, everyone?"

"To the *Hop*!"

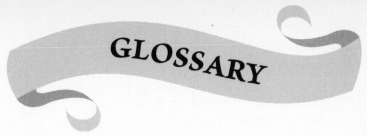
GLOSSARY

Amulet: an object worn, often as a piece of jewelry around the neck, to ward off evil

Blimey: an expression of frustration or surprise as in, "Remember when you dropped the anchor on my foot? Blimey, that hurt!"

Broadsword: a large, heavy sword with a broad blade

Buccaneer: a pirate. The term *buccaneer* comes from a French word (*boucanier*) which means "barbecuer." In the 1600s, buccaneers were humble men who sold barbecued meats to sailors passing through ports. Eventually they realized the opportunity passing them by and gave up their grills to make their fortunes by pillaging and plundering.

Careen: Cleaning the ship's hull involves beaching it, tilting it to one side, and scraping off the barnacles.

Castaway: a person lucky enough to survive a shipwreck and wash ashore, hopefully not on the Island of Smelly Wild Pigs

Crow's nest: the lookout platform near the top of a mast, not the best place for pirates afraid of heights

Cutlass: a short, curved sword with a single cutting edge, a pirate's best friend

Doubloon: a Spanish gold coin, similar to the chocolate variety, but less tasty

Drivelswigger: a pirate who spends too much time reading about all things nautical

Flotsam: floating debris or rubbish

Fo'c'sle: the raised part of the upper deck at the front of a ship, also called the forecastle

Gun deck: the deck on which the ship's cannons are carried

Jack-tar: a sailor

Keelhaul: the worst possible punishment on board a ship. The offender's hands are bound to a rope that runs underneath the ship, and he is thrown overboard and dragged from one end to the other.

Long drop: the Lost Souls' own term for the toilet

Mast: a long pole that rises from the ship's deck and supports the sails

Piece of eight: a Spanish silver coin

Plank: the piece of wood that hangs off the side of the ship, like a soon-to-be-dead-man's diving board. Unlucky sailors must walk it to their doom.

Plunder: to steal, or an act of thievery

Poop deck: the highest deck at the stern of a ship. It has nothing to do with the long drop, by the way.

Port: a sailor's word for *left*

Quarterdeck: the rear part of the upper deck at the front of a ship

Quartermaster: usually the second-in-command on a ship

Scalawag: a rascal, rogue, scoundrel, or general mischief-maker

Schooner: a ship with two or more masts. One explanation suggests that the name comes from the Scottish term "to scoon," which means "to skim upon the surface."

Scuttle: a word used by the Lost Souls to describe something awful as in, "Hardtack for breakfast again? That scuttles!"

Sloop: a small, single-mast ship

Spyglass: a much more intriguing name for a small telescope

Starboard: a sailor's word for *right*

Swain: a short form of *boatswain,* meaning a sailor of the lowest rank, more of a servant

The Hop's
hiding spot

*Ara
Rookery*

X *Lost Souls
camp*

*Ophidian's
Aggregation*

N

W   E

S

Island X

ACKNOWLEDGMENTS

Once again, I'm so lucky to have so many amazing people to thank for their support in the making of this novel. To my editors, Lynne Missen and Pamela Bobowicz, and agent, Marie Campbell: Thank you for letting the Lost Souls live on a little longer. To Catherine Marjoribanks, Melissa Zilberberg, Sarah Howden, and the entire team at HarperCollins Canada. To Fiona Pook, the talented artist behind this book's treasure map, and Tara MacDonald, creator of splendid teacher guides. To fabulous friends and colleagues who actually volunteer to read my unwieldy first drafts—namely, Ria Voros, John Mavin, Jana Fernandes, and Paul Colangelo. To Louise Delaney— always on call, red pen and words of encouragement at the ready. Thank you.

ABOUT THE AUTHOR

Photo by Shanna Baker

Rachelle Delaney lives in Vancouver, Canada, where she works as a writer, editor, and creative writing teacher. In 2010 she was named the top emerging writer in Canada by the Canadian Author's Association.

THE SHIP of LOST SOULS

THE HUNT for the PANTHER

3

by Rachelle Delaney

Coming Soon

CHAPTER ONE

"Water?"

"Check."

"Map?"

"Check."

"Empty pockets for filling with plunder?"

Jem Fitzgerald pulled his pockets inside out to show how empty they were. "Check. We're ready, Captain." He tucked his pockets back in his trousers. "We should get going."

Scarlet McCray bit her lip. "Right . . . it's just . . ." She looked up at the afternoon sky and watched a flock of green parrots flap by overhead. "I have a feeling I'm forgetting something."

Jem sighed. The captain of the Lost Souls, he knew, was not forgetting anything. She just didn't want to leave her beloved Island X. "Look, it's only for a day—" he began.

"Don't rush me, Fitz," Scarlet snapped. "I just *know* I'm forgetting something."

Jem rolled his eyes. "Okay, okay," he muttered. "Take your time then."

"I will, thanks," she retorted, crouching to retie her bootlaces.

"Fine." Jem folded his arms over his chest.

"Fine," Scarlet said to her boot.

Jem took a deep breath and counted to ten. They'd only left Island X a few times since arriving there two months before. But each time they did, Scarlet would stall until the last possible moment. He always tried to hurry her up, but there was only so much prodding the captain of the Lost Souls would take. She'd already threatened to string Tim Sanders up by his toes earlier that day when he'd called her a slowpoke. Even when she was nowhere near her ship, the captain of the Ship of Lost Souls couldn't help but act like a pirate.

Jem turned away and surveyed the lush, green clearing around them, which was slowly beginning to feel like home. Well, as much as a tropical island inhabited by smelly wild pigs, mischievous monkeys, and the odd poisonous tree *could* feel like home.

He shaded his eyes from the sun and squinted at the small but sturdy tree houses perched on the edge of the clearing. The sight of them made him stand up a little taller. As Head of the Housing Committee, he had directed the entire building project, bringing a touch of civilization to the wilds of Island X. Of course, it was nothing like his real home back in the Old World. Here, lanterns were lit by fireflies rather than flames, and everyone slept in hammocks instead of real beds. And though it was nice to hear the rain patter on their leafy rooftops at night, sturdy wooden beams would have been much more effective in keeping out curious, hungry animals. Every now and then, Jem would wake, certain he'd heard something other than birds and bugs in the trees around them. Something *big*. Something with *claws*. Something—

Scarlet grunted loudly, and Jem glanced down. She was untieing and retieing her bootlaces as if her life depended on the loops being perfectly even. He shook his head and turned back to the houses. Yes, real doors would be nice. And shutters for the windows. But those would have to wait until he returned from their trip to Port Aberhard. For whether Scarlet liked it or not, she'd been summoned to the nearby port by the only person in the world she actually had to answer to—her father.

"Blast! Blimey and bilge!" Scarlet swore as her bootlace snapped in two. "Stupid boots. Why do I have to wear them at all? They're such a waste of—" She looked up at Jem. "What?"

"What, what? I didn't say anything." He took a step back, not liking the glint in her eyes. Mad Captain McCray, as the crew sometimes called her, had a glare that made even the fiercest pirate's knees quake.

"You're giving me that look," she said, eyes narrowing.

"What look? I wasn't giving you any look," Jem protested.

"You were. It was a 'buck up, McCray, going into port's not so bad' kind of look."

"It was not," said Jem, although he suspected that was exactly the look he'd been giving her. Going into port really wasn't *that* bad.

She glared at him a moment longer, then looked down at her bootlaces and sighed. When she glanced back up, the angry look had been replaced by a downright mournful one. "I just . . . hate to leave the island," she muttered.

Jem sighed. Part of him wanted to point out that they should have been halfway to port by now. But two months under Scarlet's command had taught him that wasn't the way to get things done. He swallowed his impatience and knelt down beside her.

"Look, I know these father-daughter meetings are a pain, but look on the bright side."

Scarlet raised an eyebrow.

"Well." Jem swallowed, thinking hard. "You get to catch up on all the port news."

Scarlet looked unconvinced.

He tried again. "We can steal some of those blackberry preserves you like."

Scarlet shrugged.

Jem decided to change tactics. "It's only for one night. We'll be back tomorrow afternoon and everything will be fine. Nothing will have changed."

Two small, black monkeys scampered by, shrieking.

"For instance," he continued. "The monkeys will still be up to no good."

"Come back here!" A ginger-haired girl raced by in hot pursuit. Two purple butterflies clung to her braids, and a small chameleon poked its head out of her shirt pocket.

"And Ronagh will still be working on her menagerie," he added. Scarlet nodded and managed a tiny smile.

"And, doubtless, Smitty will still be head over heels in love." He batted his eyes at Scarlet. Finally, she laughed.

"Did I hear my name?" A tall, blond boy appeared behind them.

Jem grinned at Scarlet. "I didn't mention Horace. Did you?"

Scarlet giggled. "You mean Walter? Nope."

After several years as a Lost Soul, Smitty still refused to tell the crew his real name—"Smitty" came from "Smith," his last name. So they continued to call him by the worst names they could think of, assuming that one day, they'd guess correctly.

"We ready to go yet?" asked Smitty.

"Yes," Jem answered, just as Scarlet said, "Not quite."

Jem's shoulders sagged.

"That's fine," said Smitty. "I'll just go say good-bye to Sina one last time." He turned and trotted off across the clearing.

Jem looked Scarlet square in the eye. "Okay, Captain," he said. "If you won't do it for yourself, then do it for Sina. We need to get Smitty off this island before he drives her completely mad."

Scarlet considered this. "I heard he showed up at her tree house this morning before the sun was up and insisted on serving her breakfast. And singing all the way through."

Jem nodded. "Exactly."

Scarlet held up her hands in defeat. "All right, Fitz. You win. We'll go."

He scrambled to his feet and pulled her up before she could change her mind. But she'd only taken a few steps toward the tree houses when she stopped and raised a hand to her forehead.

"Oh no." Jem groaned under his breath. He'd been so close.

"*Shh.*" Scarlet closed her eyes for a moment. When she opened them, she announced, "It's the aras."

"Of course it is." Jem sighed.

"They need me," said Scarlet.

"Right."

"It could be important. I'll be right back. You go and gather the crew, and I'll meet you by the houses. I *will*," she added when he raised an eyebrow. "Promise."

He watched her jog off across the clearing and cursed Scarlet's favorite birds. It was entirely possible—probable, even—that they hadn't called for her at all, and she was just making one last effort to stall. But unlike Scarlet, Jem didn't have the ability to channel the island's wildlife and know when they were hungry, upset with one another, or in distress. So he couldn't say for sure.

And, anyway, the aras *were* important. Hunted to near extinction by pirates and King's Men for their beautiful red feathers, the birds were a treasure beyond everyone's expectations. They actually collected rubies, digging them out of the ground with their beaks and tucking them by the dozens inside their nests. The Lost Souls had made it their job to protect both the birds and the jewels from all the treasure-hungry pirates and King's Men in the tropics.

"Is she *still* stalling?" Tim asked, appearing at Jem's side. He pushed his spectacles up on his nose. "This is crazy!"

"She says the aras need her now," Jem said, and Tim snorted. "I know," Jem agreed. "But I think she's almost ready this time."

"That's what you said two hours ago," Tim said. He took off his spectacles, wiped them on his shirt, and then perched them on his nose again. "Can't you hurry her up?"

Jem gave him a withering look and began to walk toward the tree houses. The quartermaster always got twitchy when he'd been away from their ship, the *Margaret's Hop*, for too long. "You go find Emmett and Edwin," he called over his shoulder. "I'll grab Smitty and Liam, and we'll head off as soon as she gets back."

"Good luck with that," Tim yelled back. "Last I heard, Smitty was reciting love poems to Sina. It might take even longer to drag him away than the captain."

Jem groaned again. Getting the small crew of Lost Souls off Island X for a quick trip to port was hard enough with a reluctant captain. A lovesick crewmate, he could do without.

He found Smitty standing by himself near his tree house, watching a group play Monkey in the Middle nearby.

"Isn't she beautiful, Fitz?" Smitty said without taking his eyes off the crew.

Jem didn't have to ask who he was talking about. Smitty had been hopelessly in love with Sina since they'd first met her a few weeks before. Sina and her little brother, Kapu, were native Islanders—possibly the only two who had survived the Old World diseases the King's Men brought with them when they invaded the tropics.

"If only we could understand each other." Smitty sighed. "I've tried to talk to her like Scarlet does, with my eyes." He gave Jem an intense stare to demonstrate. "But it doesn't seem to be working."

Jem stifled a laugh. Smitty's stare was more likely to stop a smelly wild pig in its tracks than demonstrate his affections. "Well, you're not half-Islander like Scarlet is. Those two have a special connection." He couldn't quite understand it himself, but when Scarlet couldn't recall the right Islander words and Sina couldn't understand the English ones, the two friends could read each other's thoughts.

"All right, Smit. Are you ready to go?" Jem asked. But Smitty ignored him, staring at Sina until she finally turned to look his way. He waved, but the tall, dark-haired girl rolled her eyes and turned back to the game.

"Smit!" Jem snapped his fingers in front of the boy's face.

Smitty pulled his gaze away and looked at Jem. "Actually, I was thinking I might sit this trip out," he said. "Maybe I'll stay here and . . . you know." He looked dreamily at Sina again.

"Not a chance," Jem said flatly. "You're coming to port."

"But—"

"No *but*s." A little bit of Scarlet seemed to have rubbed off on him. "You love a good port raid. You're coming."

Smitty shoved his hands in his pockets. "Well, that's true. And I suppose you can't very well go without me since I am the best pickpocket in all the tropics."

"And so modest," Jem commented. But he was

heartened to hear the smart-mouthed pirate sounding a little more like his old self. Apparently, love did strange things to a person.

"Jem!" someone called. He turned to see Gil Jenkins standing near the pool in the clearing, waving both arms. "Come quick!"

"Oh, what now?" Jem groaned, jogging off. But as soon as he saw what Gil was pointing at, he began to sprint.

Two men were stumbling across the clearing, their clothes torn and filthy. "Uncle Finn!" he yelled. "Thomas! What happened?"

He hadn't seen his uncle Finn or his uncle's research assistant since they'd set off to collect plant samples a few days before. They looked like they'd been wrestling crocodiles rather than searching for the rare plant that Uncle Finn believed could cure baldness.

"Jem," Uncle Finn gasped, practically collapsing into his arms. Jem staggered under Uncle Finn's substantial weight. "Water."

"Here." Liam tossed the explorers each a canteen, which they proceeded to gulp down without even stopping to breathe.

"What the flotsam is going on?" Scarlet appeared at Jem's shoulder.

"Not sure." Jem waited for Uncle Finn to catch his breath and quench his thirst so he could start explaining. Several other Lost Souls ran over to see what the commotion was all about.

Finally, Uncle Finn handed Liam the empty canteen.

He wiped his mouth with his dirty sleeve and turned to Jem. Then he drew a deep breath. "Brace yourself, nephew," he said. "Of all the tales I've lived to tell, this one is by far the most terrifying."

A few Lost Souls gasped.

"What happened?" Jem whispered. Uncle Finn was famous for his dramatic storytelling, but this sounded dire, even for him.

"We met . . ." Uncle Finn paused dramatically. "The panther."

The Lost Souls gasped again.

"The panther?" Smitty repeated. "There's a panther on Island X?" He moved closer to Sina, putting a protective arm around her shoulders, which she quickly shrugged off. She pulled an arrow out of her bag and examined the sharpness of its point. Sina had the best aim on the island. Smitty lowered his arm and moved a few feet away.

"There is indeed." Uncle Finn sniffed. "If you'd studied my map, you'd have seen it."

"That's right!" Jem reached into his back pocket and whipped out the map. It wasn't Uncle Finn's original map, which the explorer had drawn decades ago while first exploring the islands, but a close reproduction that Jem had made himself. On the western arm of the X-shaped island, Uncle Finn had written "Panther's Lair. Hungry." Jem made a mental note to add that crucial detail to his map later. He shivered. "What happened?"

Uncle Finn dropped his voice to resume his dramatic tone. "We were out looking for more samples of the bromeliad that cures *androgenic alopecia*," he began.

"Cures what?" Ronagh piped up.

"Baldness, remember?" Scarlet told her, pointing to Uncle Finn's head of thick, curly hair. Until recently, he'd been completely bald, proving that the bromeliad really did work miracles.

Uncle Finn smoothed down his hair. "We'd hiked farther west than we'd ever gone before when we got caught in a downpour sometime yesterday evening. And then—"

"We found this hole in the side of a mountain," Thomas cut in. "Like a cave or a den. And it looked right warm and dry—"

"So we ventured in." Uncle Finn cut him off, shooting Thomas an irritated look. The old explorer preferred to tell his own tales. "Only to find ourselves face-to-face with . . ." He paused once more. "The biggest, snarliest, hungriest black panther we'd ever seen."

Several Lost Souls shrieked. A few more dove behind some larger ones for protection.

"Have you ever seen a smaller, less snarly, not-so-hungry one?" Ronagh asked.

"Quiet, Ronagh," said her brother, Liam.

"Just wondering," she muttered to the chameleon in her pocket. "Maybe there are friendlier ones."

Scarlet shook her head at the younger girl. "Don't even *think* about trying to make friends with it."

"Not on your life." Uncle Finn gave Ronagh a stern look. "We were lucky to escape with ours. And I was lucky that Thomas has the strength of ten men and could injure the beast while I made my getaway."

"You *what?*" Ronagh cried, turning to Thomas.

"I just poked 'im in the eye, real quick," Thomas said, taking a step back from the red-faced girl. "He ain't hurt, I swear!"

"But he's angry," said Uncle Finn, his eyes gleaming. "So if you value your young lives, watch out for this beast. He lives up the western arm, but who knows where he might turn up."

Jem wiped a trickle of sweat off his temple, remembering the noises he'd heard last night when everyone was asleep. Port Aberhard, with its Old World streets and buildings with doors that shut and locked, was looking better by the second.

Scarlet, however, seemed to be thinking just the opposite. "Maybe . . . maybe we shouldn't go to port today," she whispered to Jem. "Maybe we're needed here."

Jem shook his head, trying to clear it of the panther and focus on their mission. "Captain, it's already late afternoon. Your father's expecting you tonight."

"But what about the crew? We can't leave them now."

"If we leave now, we'll be back tomorrow afternoon. If we stay, we'll just have to go tomorrow. You know that," he insisted. Admiral McCray had made it clear on their last visit—when they had arrived two days late because a war broke out between two troops of monkeys—that he expected his daughter to abide by their agreement. Once every two weeks, Scarlet had to meet him in port. If she kept up her end of the bargain, he'd let her live with the Lost Souls on Island X and keep the King's Men away.

Sina slipped over and took Scarlet's arm. For a moment, they just looked at each other, and if Jem hadn't known about their strange method of communication, he would have assumed they were having an intense staring contest.

Finally, Scarlet grunted. "All right. Fine. I trust you," she said. Turning to Jem, she explained, "Sina will take care of things here until tomorrow. But we've got to go *now* so we can be back as soon as possible."

Jem let out a sigh of relief. "I'm ready. We're all ready." He tossed Sina a grateful look and turned to the small crew of travelers. "Let's get going."

CHAPTER TWO

By the time they reached the *Margaret's Hop,* the sun was close to setting. Scarlet climbed aboard, followed by Tim, Jem, Smitty, Liam, and the twins, Emmett and Edwin.

Though she'd been on board a few times in the past two months, it still felt strange to be standing on deck under the mast rather than in the jungle under a forest so thick it blocked out the sun. After all the years she'd spent away from Island X, she was finally beginning to feel like she belonged there again. She knew every tree on the edge of the clearing and every monkey that inhabited them—not to mention every monkey's problems, thanks to this newfound ability of hers to channel their thoughts.

Her first language was slow in returning, but Sina was a dedicated teacher. Every morning, she made Scarlet memorize a dozen words and forced her to use each one at least twice throughout the day.

Blimey, thought Scarlet, *I'm going to miss tomorrow's lesson. I should have asked Sina for a dozen words to practice by myself. Now I'll be behind, and I'll—*

"We'll be back tomorrow afternoon," Jem reminded her, appearing at her side. "And nothing will have changed."

She shook herself back to the present. "Right. Yes. I know."

Jem handed her some nuts he'd brought along with him. "If you don't mind my saying, Captain," he said, "sometimes it's best to stop thinking and just . . . do."

Scarlet gulped down her nuts. He was right, as usual. She had a mission to complete. It was time to act like a captain.

She looked around. "Emmett and Edwin, weigh anchor!" she yelled at the twins. "Tim, take the wheel, and, Smit, mind the mast. Liam, this deck looks like bilge—swab it quick, will you? And, Fitz?" She turned to him. "Check the ropes for frays, and replace the worst ones."

Jem nodded and saluted. "Yes, Captain!" He set off to check the ropes.

Good old Fitz, she thought, watching the boy march off in his surprisingly clean trousers and boots. *What would I do without him?*

Soon they were out in the open ocean, sailing east toward Port Aberhard, away from the setting sun. Scarlet took a deep breath of cool, salty air, then another. Life on board the *Hop* wasn't so bad. In fact, it had been a jolly home for two years, just when she'd needed it most. She owed all she knew about being a pirate to this old boat and its crew.

She ran her hand along the weathered railing, suddenly ashamed at having neglected the *Hop*. Tim was constantly pointing out new holes in her sides and rips in her mast. "Thank you," Scarlet whispered, patting the railing.

She walked across the main deck and up to the fo'c'sle,

leaning over the edge to watch a pair of glowing jellyfish bobbing in the water below. Then she dug around in her pocket for Uncle Finn's old spyglass and pressed it to her eye, scanning the horizon for approaching ships.

"See anything?" Tim yelled from the ship's wheel, where he studied a map and compass.

"Not a speck, Swig," Scarlet called back. Tim's love of nautical books and maps had earned him the nickname "Drivelswigger," or "Swig" for short. "Too bad—it would have been a nice night for a ship raid."

"Doubt we'll be able to get away with raiding anymore, Captain," Tim replied, and Scarlet lowered the spyglass. She'd forgotten, but Tim was right.

The legend of the Ship of Lost Souls had begun some ten years before, when a ship had set out carrying a class of geography students and schoolmasters from a port school. They'd gotten themselves lost in a hurricane, and when they eventually found their way home, they learned that not only had they been presumed dead, but that sailors who spotted their ship believed it to be haunted by ghosts. They called it The Ship of Lost Souls.

Instead of setting them straight, the children decided to play along, dressing up like ghouls in long, black cloaks and swooping down on the ships of pirates and King's Men when they needed food or supplies. The ship soon became a magnet for children orphaned in the tropics or running away from boarding schools or ships—or, in Scarlet's case, home.

"The legend had a good run," said Edwin, joining her and Tim at the wheel.

"Suppose it had to die sooner or later." Emmett sighed.

Scarlet grunted. "It'd still be alive and well if it weren't for that dog Lucas Lawrence, leaving to join a 'real' pirate ship." She still couldn't help but sneer whenever she thought of her former crew member.

"He's a bilge rat," said Emmett.

"A scurvy swine," Tim spat.

Scarlet nodded. Those were the only ways to describe someone who'd not only defected from the Lost Souls but told his new crew the Lost Souls' secret. Now everyone knew that they were just children. Brave and strong and clever children, of course, but children nonetheless.

"Wonder what old Lucas is up to now," said Edwin.

"No good," Scarlet answered with complete certainty. Lucas had taken off with Uncle Finn's map, so he knew exactly where the treasure was. He and his new crew from the *Dark Ranger* had tried to steal it once and would certainly try again soon. It was just a matter of time. "Can we hurry?" she asked Tim.

He frowned at her over his spectacles.

"Sorry," she muttered. Sometimes a good captain had to know when to leave her quartermaster to do his job.

She picked up the spyglass again and forced herself to not look back at Island X. Instead she looked forward, at their destination, where she'd soon be meeting her father. These father-daughter meetings truly scuttled, but she'd take Jem's advice and stop thinking about them. She'd just answer her father's questions and assure him that all was well on Island X. Then she'd be back on board the *Hop* and sailing home in no time.

She reached out and tapped the wooden railing for good luck. Just in case.

"Smit, quit splashing me," Liam complained.

"Splashing? Who's splashing?" Smitty said innocently. After dropping anchor in the bay near Port Aberhard, they had all piled into their dinghy to row ashore. Smitty had insisted he take the oars.

"Argh! He did it again! Scarlet!"

"*Shh*. Quiet, Liam," Scarlet whispered. The last thing they needed was the attention of some pirates or King's Men. "One more time, Leander, and I'm tossing you overboard," she warned Smitty.

"Then who would row us to port?" said Smitty. Despite the darkness, Scarlet could tell he was grinning.

"Me," Edwin volunteered.

"I'd do it," said Tim.

"Or me," Jem offered.

"Oh, so I'm that replaceable, am I?" Smitty *tsk*ed. "Fine then, I'll just—"

"Argh! Again!" Liam cried as Smitty's oar flicked seawater up into his face. "That's it! I'm gonna pound you!"

"Liam, sit down, you're rocking the boat!" Scarlet commanded.

"Hey!" A voice shouted from nearby. The crew froze, then slowly looked to the right, where a grizzled old sailor stood in a rowboat, holding up a lantern. "What's goin' on there? Who are ye?"

"Tim!" Scarlet hissed, for she couldn't very well answer herself.

"Just some cabin boys, sir," Tim called. "Heading in to port for the night."

"Well, get on with ye," the sailor told them. "'Cause I sure ain't gonna rescue ye when ye capsize."

"Yes, sir!" Tim called.

Scarlet kicked Smitty. "Row!"

"Bilge rat," Liam added under his breath, but Smitty pretended he hadn't heard.

They made it to the docks without capsizing and scrambled out of the boat, which Tim tied to a post. Already Scarlet could hear the raucous sounds of port: shouts and hollers from some drunken pirates, tinny piano music from a nearby tavern, and the crunch of heavy boots on gravel. She tried not to think about the insect and ara orchestra that played all through the night on Island X, lulling everyone to sleep.

"Come on, crew," she said once they were all up on the dock. "Let's get this over with."

The only good thing about being in port was that children were rarely noticed. The pirates were too busy insulting and spitting at one another, and the King's Men were too busy trying to look important and keep their blue uniforms spotless. Which made it nice and easy for the Lost Souls to nab what they needed and disappear before anyone knew they were there.

"All right." Scarlet motioned for the crew to duck into an alley, where they huddled in the shadows. "We need some food—Edwin and Emmett, I'll leave that to you. Jem, get whatever supplies you need to finish the houses. Tim and Liam, you're on weapons—Charlie and Gil need new daggers. Oh, and some shirts and trousers. Smit, that'll be your—" She stopped when she caught sight of Smitty's face. The boy was chewing on his lower lip. "What now?" she growled.

Smitty sighed. "Well, if you must know, I just saw a piece of rope, and it reminded me of the way Sina braids her hair some days, and I—"

"Smitty!" Tim threw his hands in the air. "We're on a port raid! We've got things to plunder, pockets to pick! This is no time to be a swoony sea dog!"

"Wait. I know," Jem said. "Smit, why don't you find a gift for Sina? You know, something nice. While you're stealing the other stuff, that is."

Smitty perked up immediately. "That's a jolly idea, Fitz. Maybe I'll get her something for her hair. One of those . . . clip thingies."

Scarlet opened her mouth to point out that a gift he'd actually paid for might be more thoughtful, then shook her head. There was no time to argue. "Right. Good luck with that," she said. "Let's meet back at the dock in a few hours."

She put her fist in the middle of their huddle, and the others, who knew the tradition well, piled theirs on top of it. "No prey, no pay, mateys."

"No prey, no pay!" they echoed.

"May you die peacefully on Island X rather than have your hands chopped off by the merchants you stole from."

"Die peacefully!"

"Now get going," said Scarlet. "I've got an admiral to meet."

Scarlet made sure all her hair was tucked inside her cap and pulled it down over her eyes before slipping out of the alley. This way, if one of the King's Men spotted her father during their meeting, he'd assume the admiral was talking to some scruffy cabin boy and not his long-lost daughter.

She headed down Port Aberhard's main road, past a tavern packed with rum-soaked pirates singing off-key chanteys. She passed an apothecary's shop boarded up for the night and sidestepped a pack of rats squealing over scraps outside the door. She could smell the jungle nearby, but its lush scent was overpowered by port smells like sour rum, horse manure, and rotting wood.

If there was one place in the tropics that did not and would never feel like home, it was Port Aberhard. Or any port town, for that matter. Not even Jamestown, where she'd lived for five years, felt remotely like home.

Her father had taken her to Jamestown after the Island Fever came to their village when she was five years old. Scarlet's mother had begged her father to take her off the island and keep her safe from the disease that was taking many Islander lives—including, eventually, her mother's. They'd settled in a rickety old boardinghouse, and John McCray had gone back to work for the King's Men, leaving Scarlet to learn Old World ways from the world's creepiest governess, whom she called Scary Mary. After five years of English lessons, petticoats, and boots that pinched her toes until she was certain they'd fall off, she decided she'd had enough and ran away to join the Lost Souls.

Even now, port towns made Scarlet's skin crawl. It wasn't just the memories of Scary Mary forcing her to forget her past as an Islander that haunted her. It was more than that. The longer she lived on Island X, the more she felt the island's pain at being torn down and taken apart by the Old Worlders. And nowhere was that more pronounced than in port.

Don't think about it now, Scarlet told herself. *Get to your meeting, then get home to the crew.*

Dodging a pair of pirates stumbling toward her, she continued on, looking for the tiny clapboard house her father had described.

Admiral McCray insisted on holding each of their meetings in a secret location—someplace the other King's Men would never think to look for him. Last time they'd met in the cellar of a tavern, which was freezing cold and crawling with spiders. This time, however, he'd chosen someplace he insisted would be better: Voodoo Miranda's house.

It stood near the end of the street, squeezed between two ramshackle brick buildings. Scarlet paused out front and swallowed hard. Every window was dark, but that didn't mean the voodoo queen wasn't home. She was probably cooking up some potion that would turn an unsuspecting person into a two-headed lizard.

Stop thinking, Scarlet told herself again. *Just do.* She gathered all the courage she could find, stepped up to the rotting door, and knocked twice.

Even though she'd seen Voodoo Miranda several times over the years, she still jumped when the front door swung open and the woman peered out, baring her crooked teeth. Easily six feet tall, Voodoo Miranda wore a long green dress that glimmered in the light of the twisted black candle she held. She had long, matted black hair that hung down to her waist, and her lips were painted a deep purple.

But that wasn't the worst of it. Coiled around her left wrist, like a big poisonous bracelet, was a shiny green python. Another snake, this one a striped viper, was nestled in her enormous hair, watching Scarlet closely.

Scarlet took a hasty step back, wiping her sweaty palms on her trousers. She hated snakes, especially the small ones that looked harmless but could kill you with one bite. "Um. Hello."

Voodoo Miranda squinted at her for a moment. Then her mouth spread into a wide purple smile. "Come in."

She stepped aside, and Scarlet darted past into a room full of dusty furniture that probably hadn't been used for years. There were black candles everywhere, and the loose floorboards creaked underfoot. Scarlet couldn't help but wonder if Voodoo Miranda hid something underneath them. Or someone . . .

Stop! she told herself. "Um, where am I meeting him?"

"In the kitchen," said Miranda. "This way." She led

Scarlet down a pitch-dark hallway into another room—this one lit by a single lantern. The kitchen was cluttered with bottles and jars of every size and color, and it smelled like long-dead flowers that had never been tossed out.

"Don't mind my work," Voodoo Miranda said, gesturing at some mounds of wax on the table.

"Work?" Scarlet stepped closer. One of the mounds had a distinctly human shape. *A voodoo doll,* she realized, just as Miranda snatched it up and tucked it into her pocket. She'd heard sailors whisper that if you ever needed to get revenge, Voodoo Miranda could help. She'd whip up a little wax doll that looked just like your enemy in the time it took you to say "scalawag." Then she'd stick little pins in the doll's back and ears, and the unfortunate person would be keeling over in pain in no time.

"Sit." Miranda pointed to a chair, and Scarlet obeyed, finding herself staring into the eyes of a long-dead frog, floating wide-eyed in a jar of yellow liquid. When Miranda wasn't looking, she quickly turned the jar so the creature was facing away from her.

"Make yourself comfortable," Miranda said.

"Thanks," Scarlet said weakly.

"Ah. Think I hear your father," said Miranda.

"Really? I didn't hear anything," Scarlet replied, but Miranda had already slipped back out the door.

"Huh," Scarlet muttered, peering into a jar on the counter, which appeared to hold several hundred small, green beetles. "What does a voodoo queen eat, anyway?"

Fortunately, before she could find the answer to

that question, the door swung open again, and Admiral McCray walked into the room.

"Scarlet!" He stopped and took off his blue cap, a wide smile spreading across his face. She stood up and let him pull her into a warm hug. For the tiniest moment, she even let herself relax, enjoying the feeling of having someone around to take care of her. But then she felt Miranda's eyes on her back, and she wiggled out of her father's arms. The voodoo queen was watching them intently, stroking her python's head.

"Thank you, Miranda," said the admiral. "We won't be long."

Miranda nodded. "There are cookies on the counter if you get hungry." She narrowed her eyes at Scarlet. "Looks like you could use a good meal."

"I just ate," Scarlet said quickly, although it had been several hours since she'd snacked on the nuts Jem had packed. If the jars around the kitchen were any indication of the ingredients Miranda baked with, she'd rather pass.

Miranda shrugged and slipped away again, leaving Scarlet and her father alone.

Even now, it still surprised her to see him. Not that he'd changed much in their time apart; she'd known him the moment she saw him on Island X, about a month before. He'd arrived with his men, scouting the island for untouched resources, and she'd quickly realized that he'd completely forgotten everything about the island—he didn't even recognize it as the place he'd called home for years.

"Please, sit down." He gestured to her chair, and she sat

again. He picked up his cap, then set it back down on the table. "So."

"So," she said.

"Are the tree houses finished now?"

"Almost," she replied. "They look jolly—Fitz did a great job."

"And the garden?"

"Done. Gil took a real shine to weeding and planting. Sina thinks we'll have squash in a month or so."

The admiral nodded and fiddled with his cap. "And no sign of that pirate captain . . . what's his name again?"

Scarlet shook her head. The Dread Pirate Captain Wallace Hammerstein-Jones led the *Dark Ranger*, the ship Lucas Lawrence defected to. He was just as treasure hungry as Lucas himself, which meant more trouble for the Lost Souls since Lucas had Uncle Finn's treasure map. Scarlet tapped her feet on the floor, her thoughts flitting back to her crew. Hopefully her father wouldn't keep her long.

"Speaking of captains," her father continued, "do you have a plan to stop this new one from getting the treasure?"

Scarlet started. "What new one?"

The admiral looked down at the frog in the jar and noticed it for the first time. He grimaced and turned it so it faced the wall.

"The new pirate captain," he repeated. "Surely you've heard of him."

Scarlet leaned forward. This sounded serious. "Fill me in."

The admiral frowned. "Everyone's talking about him, though, I have yet to meet anyone who has actually met him. Apparently a new pirate is rising to power, and he's gathering a crew of the filthiest and fiercest pirates around. Rumor has it he aims to be the most powerful pirate in all the tropics."

"What?" Scarlet cried, then lowered her voice. "What does that mean?"

The admiral frowned. "Well, he wants the most powerful crew, the fastest and biggest ship, and control of all the treasure around."

"Shivers!" Scarlet tried to imagine it. Then she started as another thought came to mind. "What if Lucas decides to join him? He's got the map!"

"My thoughts exactly," said her father. "He's just the type to—"

Voodoo Miranda poked her head into the kitchen. "Hungry yet?" she asked, narrowing her eyes at Scarlet.

"Oh no!" Scarlet said. "I'm full." She patted her stomach, which proceeded to growl.

"Just as I thought," Miranda insisted, sweeping through the door. The striped viper was still nestled in her hair, but the snake on her wrist was nowhere to be seen. Scarlet glanced around nervously. "Baked them last week." Miranda grabbed a plate piled high with small gray lumps off the counter and thrust them at Scarlet.

"Oh, I couldn't—"

"Try them!" Miranda pushed the plate toward her.

Scarlet snatched up a gray lump and took a nibble. It tasted salty and a bit like the hardtack the Lost Souls used to eat on board the *Hop*. But there was something else . . . some flavor she couldn't quite put her finger on.

"Um . . . what kind of cookies are they?"

Miranda wiggled her eyebrows. "I call them 'rodent surprises.' The snakes love them."

Scarlet's mouth fell open and she looked down at her half-eaten cookie. Sure enough, she could make out the tip of a tiny, hairless tail sticking out. She gagged and sputtered. Miranda was watching her closely, as was the viper in Miranda's hair. It took all her willpower to swallow.

"It's good," Scarlet told them weakly.

Miranda straightened and gave her a crooked smile. "I know," she said, and slipped back out the door.

Scarlet swallowed hard again and turned back to her father. "Look, I can't stay much longer. I've got to get back to my crew, especially now that I know about this captain. We'll need another plan now to protect the island." She stood and pushed back her chair.

The admiral checked his pocket watch. "Wait," he said. "There's one more thing I have to tell you."

"About the captain?"

"Well, no. This is . . . something different."

Scarlet sat back down and watched him fiddle with his cap again. A pit began to grow in her stomach. Could there be even *worse* news?

"Your uncle Daniel is coming for a visit. From the Old World."

Scarlet cocked her head to the side. "My what?"

"Your uncle Daniel," he repeated. "My older brother. You've never met him."

"Oh," Scarlet said, wondering what the flotsam this had to do with her.

"He won't be staying long. Three weeks at most, and he'll be bringing his daughter, who's your age. Her name is Josephine."

Oh. Scarlet stayed quiet, hoping this wasn't leading where she suspected it might be.

"Daniel is a very high-ranking King's Man. In fact, he's a deputy advisor to King Aberhard himself."

"Mmm-hmm," said Scarlet.

"When we moved away from the Island after the fever, he used his power to get me a position again. They would have never taken me back otherwise."

"Because God forbid you'd gone off and married an Islander," Scarlet finished, rolling her eyes. She despised the King's Men and all their Old World ideas.

The admiral paused. "Daniel means well," he said carefully. "He doesn't understand the tropics. He's only ever advised from afar. But he's my brother, and he's always taken care of me. So when you disappeared, I . . . I didn't tell him. I knew he'd be on the first ship over to search for you. It would have turned my family upside-down."

This only went to prove Scarlet's theory that grown-ups made no sense. If you couldn't call them for help because they'll only make more trouble, what good are they? But she stayed quiet, the pit in her stomach growing bigger.

"The point is, I need you to stay in port with me," he finished.

Scarlet's mouth fell open. "You want . . . what?"

The admiral nodded. "It'll be about three weeks. A deputy advisor couldn't be away from the king for any longer than a few months."

"*Three weeks?*" Scarlet couldn't believe her ears. "Father, you've got to be joking! I can't leave the island for three *weeks*."

The admiral frowned. "Believe me, Scarlet, I've thought this through. We have no choice here. I cannot have my brother finding out that you live by yourself on another island. He wouldn't understand."

"But—"

"And what's more, it could be dangerous. Daniel's loyalty lies first and foremost with the king, and if he were to find out about Island X and its treasure—the very treasure King Aberhard is looking for—I'd hate to think what he'd have to do."

Scarlet swallowed hard. "Can't you tell him I'm at boarding school?"

Her father shook his head. "He'd insist we go visit you. Trust me, Scarlet, there is no way around this."

Scarlet fought the rising panic in her throat by swallowing hard. "When are they coming?"

"Their ship docks tomorrow."

"*Tomorrow?*" she cried. "You've got to be joking! My crew—"

"Will survive without you for three weeks," he finished. "They're smart and strong and nothing will go wrong in your absence."

"But—"

"Scarlet." This time his voice was heavy, and she knew there was no use arguing any more. "Sometimes we have to do things we don't want to do. Sometimes that's what having a family is all about."

And that just absolutely scuttled.